KU-691-926

First published in Great Britain in 2015 by Comma Press
www.commapress.co.uk

A CIP catalogue record of this book is available from the British Library.

ISBN 1905583575
ISBN-13 978 1905583577

The publisher gratefully acknowledges the support of Arts Council England.

The Book of Tokyo was developed as a joint project of Comma Press, the British Centre for Literary Translation and the Nippon Foundation.

Set in Bembo 11/13 by David Eckersall
Printed and bound by CPI Group (UK) Ltd, Croydon, CR0 4YY

The Book of Tokyo

Edited by
Michael Emmerich,
Jim Hinks
& Masashi Matsuie

Contents

CONTENTS

Introduction

NOT SO VERY LONG ago, descriptions of Tokyo – sections of the city, real landmarks, parks, alleys, movie theatres – appeared almost as a matter of course in works of Japanese literature. The very first sentence of the book often considered 'Japan's first modern novel,' Futabatei Shimei's *Drifting Cloud* (*Ukigumo*, 1887-1889), opens with a description of a crowd of men streaming through a particular gate in Tokyo onto the street outside, displaying every manner of modern moustache and beard, each scrupulously trimmed. Tellingly, while the gate is named, no mention is made of its being in Tokyo; Futabatei simply assumes the reader will recognise it, or at least presume that it must be in Tokyo. After all, Tokyo was the capital, and to a large extent modern literature itself was a phenomenon of the capital. Even fiction that was not set in Tokyo often brimmed with a keen awareness of this fact – of the distance that separated peripheral settings from the centre – and thus functioned as a sort of mirror image of the metropolis that did not figure in it. *La literature*, Tokyo might have said, *c'est moi*.

This is hardly a surprise, given that for as long as it has existed, more authors have called Tokyo home than any other city in Japan, and that throughout the modern period Tokyo has been the unchallenged centre of the publishing industry. Indeed, the city's literary dominance can be traced back even before its rebirth as 'Tokyo' in 1868, to an age when it was still called 'Edo', and served as the bureaucratic capital of early modern Japan – the counterpart of the ancient imperial capital of Kyoto. Early in the seventeenth century, Edo had been little more than a sparsely populated swamp; by the dawn of the eighteenth century its population had shot past one million, making it the largest metropolis in the world – larger even than Beijing, almost twice the size of London. With its highly-developed economy, and a population with significantly higher literacy rates than London, Edo had proved itself exceptionally fertile ground for popular culture, including various genres of illustrated fiction, printed from woodblocks, that Edoites proudly called 'local books.'

Only once in the past two centuries has the city ever seemed in danger of losing its position of leadership in the world of Japanese literary production. In the aftermath of the Great Kantō Earthquake of 1923, the major publishing houses were rumoured to be on the verge of abandoning the ruined city for Osaka. In the end, they decided to stay; the only significant literary loss Tokyo suffered was that of Tanizaki Jun'ichirō, who moved his household to Kyoto. So many writers lived, and continue to live in Tokyo and its suburbs, that this move has come to be remembered as a noteworthy event, not only in Tanizaki's life, but in Japanese literary history itself. Apart from that one incident, as one surveys Japanese literature from the mid 1880s to the early 1970s, situating this modern history within the larger sweep of Japanese literature from the end of the early modern period, it is hard not to succumb to a feeling akin to the bewildered awe Sanshirō experienced in Natsume Sōseki's famous novel *Sanshirō* (1908). When the hero first arrived in Tokyo, after a three-day train trip from Kumamoto, on the island of Kyūshū, 'The thing that most surprised him, the narrator says, 'was that no matter how far you went, Tokyo never ended.'

And yet, what do we find when we turn to the contemporary scene? As in earlier decades, countless novels and stories are set in Tokyo – many more than take place in any other part of Japan, be it another city or the countryside, or, for that matter, in other regions of the world. Tokyo remains the centre of publishing and home to the majority of Japan's writers. But there has been a fairly pronounced tendency, at least in one prominent strand of contemporary Japanese literature, to turn away from an engagement with the particularities of Tokyo's urban landscape – to retreat altogether, indeed, from the realities of place. From time to time, of course, we encounter the names of actual streets and buildings, shops, subway lines and parks, but even when we do, the proper nouns often seem subtly detached from the physical world. This is perfectly symbolised by a scene in Hitomi Kanehara's story 'Mambo,' which appears in this anthology in translation by Dan Bradley. The narrator tells a man she has just met that she is on her way to 'Seaside Park,' just as he is, and they decide to share a taxi. Once they get in the car, however, the driver points out that there are several Seaside Parks in Tokyo. Neither of the passengers knew this, or has any idea which of these various parks they want to go to; eventually, the man tells the driver, 'Any one is fine so, for the time being, please just take us to Seaside Park.' Kanehara's Tokyo is *sous rature*; a place of discomposure and disorientation: 'I wondered at that moment if it was possible that I was not actually in a taxi at all, but elsewhere…'

To be sure, some of the stories in this anthology do feel more connected to the ambiance of certain explicitly named areas of the city – West Ikebukuro in Toshiyuki Horie's 'The Owl's Estate' (translated by Jonathan Lloyd-Davies) and Shūichi Yoshida's 'An Elevator on Sunday' (translated by Ginny Tapley Takemori), for instance – or at least a certain type of area, such as the 'suburb... only twenty minutes by rail or subway from the city centre,' that comes alive so magnificently in Hiromi Kawakami's 'The Hut on the Roof' (translated by Lucy Fraser). But still, this is a far cry from the sort of experience we have when we read Natsume Sōseki's *Kokoro* (1914), for instance: there are moments in this novel when Sōseki almost seems to be encouraging us to take out a map and plot the walks Sensei takes – or rather, Sōseki seems to assume we could trace Sensei's footsteps as he stalks through the city in our minds, without any need of a map. The gravity of a book like *Kokoro* is intimately bound up with the familiar geography, the real landscape, of Tokyo. The contemporary short story is different. In a sense, you might say that the stories of this anthology unfold within a landscape more imagined than real – that they create a Tokyo of their own by drawing on a rather abstract sense of the moods of certain sections of the city, or on a vision of Tokyo and the smaller areas it comprises that is more conceptual than physical. Hideo Furukawa's 'Model T Frankenstein' (translated by Samuel Malissa) is the most concentrated expression of this tendency: in it, Tokyo becomes an almost unreal abstraction precisely because Tokyo – or more to the point, the desire to escape or to destroy the very feeling of bewildered awe that Tokyo's endlessness impressed upon Sanshirō – is its most important theme.

The sense of detachment from the physical cityscape that characterizes this collection is one thing that distinguishes the stories it contains from literature of an earlier age. Another is the position they occupy *as stories* in the larger literary field. Recent decades have witnessed something of a decline in the popularity of short stories in Japan, in part because the most prominent literary award – the Akutagawa Prize – tends to go to novellas. And so, in contrast to stories of an earlier age, which had the air of settled belonging typical of a long-term resident in an old apartment building, these stories seem comfortable with a life of roaming. There is a kind of freedom in them, a willingness to pause, to wander, to take an unexpected turn, that derives, at least in part, from the very fact that the market doesn't care as much for short stories as it used to. Exciting things happen in less popular forms.

The stories in this anthology are also diverse, despite their focus on Tokyo and the overlapping of certain other themes. This is true not only of the content, but of the authors, who include writers of various ages, from their early thirties to their late sixties; authors who have written both 'literary' and 'genre' fiction, and six women and four men.

Reading *The Book of Tokyo*, you may not always be able to identify your location on a map. If so, it means you are getting there – you are experiencing one of the great pleasures of being in Tokyo: a sense of disorientation that blends seamlessly into a seemingly opposite sense of rootedness, of being at home. You can live in Tokyo all your life and feel that you have been moving constantly.

Michael Emmerich, Feb 2015

Model T Frankenstein

Hideo Furukawa

Translated by Samuel Malissa

YOU SEE A GOAT.

You did not expect there to be a goat, so you are surprised. But what you see before you is not just one goat – there are several goats. A quick count tells you there are five or six.

The goats are fenced in.

But it cannot quite be called a fence can it?

No, you don't think so.

It's just several white planks sticking out of the ground.

These make up a vague sort of enclosure.

Something inside could escape if it wanted to. Within this – fence? non-fence? – are the goats.

The ground is green.

Grass, of course.

Further away the terrain slopes downward, eventually becoming a cliff that drops off into the sea.

So within your field of vision are both the goats and the sea behind them.

That is when you remember – *I'm on an island.*

This is an island fifty minutes by plane from Tokyo.

But what does that mean, *from Tokyo?* This island is still within the boundaries of the Tokyo metropolitan area. Mailing addresses here include 'Tokyo', which is just one way to know that this is not part of any other prefecture. There is a certain vagueness in this too – a very common sort of vagueness.

For example, 'fifty minutes by plane from Tokyo' is incorrect.

Because this is still Tokyo.

From Haneda Airport, then.

You lose yourself in the act of observing.

The goats feel your gaze on them.

The goats can sense you there.

So they begin to move about, inside of the fence (or non-fence).

The ones lying down get up. They get up, and while before there was nothing in particular to draw their attention, now they have noticed *you* – and they begin to urinate.

It is a tremendous amount of urine.

And then they defecate, great heaps of dung.

But there is no glimmer of life.

They have a mechanical feel – they had to rouse themselves, and so they did.

They give off the impression of being artificial life-forms.

Is this what it means for a living creature to be kept and raised?

You don't know.

But you feel sad.

On this island, on the grass by the cliffside that overlooks the sea, there are goats – enclosed and yet not enclosed, but without a doubt domesticated.

Now you realise that there are more than just five or six goats.

The ones that had been lying down have stood up.

You appeared, and so they had no choice but to stand up.

You find this overwhelmingly sad.

Unbearably so.

The goats hardly make any noise. They seem to have nothing to say. They have no one they could say anything to.

You think, *They really are artificial life forms.*

All of these goats are artificial.

Then, one by one, the goats come toward you, drawing closer, meeting your eye between the slats of the fence, but giving no indication of having anything to express to you. It is as if they are simply following orders.

But these are not your orders.

As you stand there being watched by the goats, you are gripped with the sense that you are about to disappear.

And in fact, you are disappearing.

You are almost completely gone.

You exist, now, solely in the act of observation.

One by one, the goats fall back.

There is no master to give them orders, so they retreat.

Then they urinate.

Then they defecate.

There is not one iota of feeling, nothing vital within them. Nonetheless, having woken up, the goats begin to eat. There is feed on the ground – you see that it is plant matter, the cut up stalks and leaves of ashitaba.[1]

There for the eating.

Raw.

You find it surprising that these domesticated goats are fed on ashitaba.

At this point you realise that, a short way off from that indeterminate enclosure (is it a fence? or a non-fence?), a lone goat stands motionless.

This goat has been looking at you for quite some time now.

You look back. It is a male goat. His horns are different than those of the others – much bigger, and stoutly curved. He is clearly a fully-grown goat.

1. Plant indigenous to the island of Hachijō, used in folk remedies as well as for grazing. The name, meaning 'tomorrow's leaf', stems from its regenerative powers: harvesting it at dawn results in new sprouts the next day.

But you do not know why this lone adult male has been forced apart from the others.

He is tied to something.

There is a rope around his neck.

This lone he-goat, separated from the flock.

But the rope is not tied to a tree. Rather it is tightly bound around a heavy piece of lumber, a huge slab of wood. If he could drag that behind him, he could move about freely.

As you observe, he begins to move towards you.

But there is nothing threatening about this. He is simply moving, in the same automatic way that the other goats stood up.

He tries to approach you, pulling at the weight, that mass of solid wood.

It's heavy.

It prevents him from continuing forward.

Instead, he ends up veering off to the right.

The he-goat can only move in an orbit around the weight.

Though he's trying to get closer to you, he is drawn inexorably to the right, plodding onwards. When he has made a half circle around his anchor, he is facing the sea.

It's a sad way to move.

It's a sad way to live.

From the start, the goat has been unable to see you.

You who have disappeared, you who now exist only in the act of observing.

But the goat felt your presence.

He felt your gaze on him.

And so he started moving.

But all he could see was the sea, and the weight was as heavy as always.

The goat knows that he is not free.

You do not know this. Or perhaps you just realised it, and are now bewildered.

There are ashitaba leaves on the ground for the male goat as well.

They are cut and piled there for him to eat.

He eats them.

The leaves are full of all kinds of nutrients. Not just rich in fibre and potassium, but protein, vitamin E, vitamin B complex, calcium, carotene, and more. Of course the goat has no idea about these nutrients. But when he eats something that is good for him, he knows it. You do not know this.

Because you are nothing more than an observer.

Your existence is transparent.

Or else... yes, that's right, it's because you have no connection to this particular Tokyo. You might say that you do not know, because this is a tertiary Tokyo.

Here on the southernmost island of the (so-called) Izu Islands, you are ignorant in the extreme.

You know nothing whatsoever.

Now the goat lifts up his head.

This time he is determined to meet the gaze he feels.

He is determined to see the gazer.

But no matter how he strains to see what's between him and the sea, he cannot detect any signs of life. There is no living flesh to speak of. *It might just be a spirit*, thinks the goat. But he does not put these thoughts into words. Goats do not have language like human beings do. When he thinks, 'It might just be a spirit,' he can only think it as a form of sensation.

All he is certain of is that there is something transparent there.

That see-through observer is you.

In your extreme ignorance, you begin to move. This time you are the one moving toward the goat. But it cannot exactly be described as moving. This is because the goat is the only one here with a body that can move. There is no you; you are nothing more than a spirit.

And the goat is thinking.

He is thinking without language (or perhaps in a primordial language). He is trying to speak aloud. All he can manage is a faint bleating. He is sad about something.

Look up – the sky.

There are contrails from passing planes.

There is an airport on this island. It is called Hachijō Airport.

Look up at a different angle – the mountain.

Originally the goats (the he-goat, and the others besides) would have lived on the skirt of the mountain. It rises from the ocean to the cliffs, and then further on until the peak, at first climbing steeply and then at a more gentle slope, this mountain that is actually a dormant volcano. At 854 metres above sea level, the summit is the highest point on the Izu Archipelago.

The he-goat turns away from the mountain. He looks at the sea, dotted with islets. These are the Little Islands of Hachijō .

There is the Japan Current.

There are the salty breezes.

The goat feels the caress of the sea air.

Or maybe it is just wind with salt in it. He can no longer feel your gaze; you are far too insubstantial. And yet you watch: the goat cannot walk another step with his burden. There is wild aloe growing here and there among the grass, but the goat shows no interest in it. He once more begins eating ashitaba. The raw ashitaba is there for him to eat. The stalks. The leaves.

Then he urinates.

Then he defecates.

Then it begins to rain, and he stands there getting wet.

Twice a day there are squalls on the island, and the goat has no choice but to stand out in the rain.

Water drips from his long, curved horns.

Rainwater. He sees it. You see it too. But you are not there. You are far too ignorant. In your existence that is only observation; your interest in this tertiary Tokyo is fading. Observing is an action that you can lose yourself in, but is existence… is existence an action?

These sorts of questions do not occur to you.

Because, as has been established, you are completely ignorant, and intermittently stupefied. Tertiary Tokyo has a tertiary Tokyo night, and a dawn, and a morning. It is the morning of tertiary Tokyo. You greet the morning, but you are nothing more than a spirit. The goat is the subject, the one experiencing all of this. You are watching, but watching is all you can do. So watch. This morning the goat is captured. He is captured alive, taken and loaded onto the flatbed of a truck. But isn't it inaccurate to say captured in the case of a goat that is already domesticated? Isn't it true that the basic premise of domestication is in being kept captive and alive by humans (that is, by the human animal, by *homo sapiens*)?

You don't ask whose head it is, where these questions are floating around.

The goat is a model of obedience as he is loaded onto the flatbed. A ride some 30 minutes up the overland road and he is delivered to the wharf, where he is unloaded and transferred into a shipping container. This container is specially designed for transporting live animals. The doors close on him. They are made of metal and won't easily be forced open. And there on the inside is the he-goat, alone. The special container has a device that the goat can press his head against to get drinking water, and the floor is covered in ashitaba. There's a ventilation system too. He is imprisoned there, giving the impression of being an artificial life form, which is to say a machine. He has flesh, he eliminates waste, he ingests food, he calls out (bleats) when he wants to and does not call out (bleat) when he doesn't feel like it. The thing inside the container cannot see outside, nor can the observer outside see in. But take a good look at what you can see. A forklift is moving the container. The tightly sealed metal box is loaded into the hold of a ferry. The ferry leaves Hachijō, probably headed north. It'll probably follow a direct course up the Izu Archipelago towards Tokyo Bay. But it's not trying to get to a port in Tokyo. Saying that would be a mistake, because Hachijō itself is a port in Tokyo. Saying otherwise would be inappropriate. And in this situation, saying something inappropriate is a mistake. It's appropriate to stress this point. It's Tokyo. It's Tokyo.

From the southern tip of the Izu Islands, the next island to the north is Tokyo. The ferry is headed there now. This island has sheer cliffs and a dormant volcano 851 metres tall (only three metres shorter than the tallest peak in the Izu islands). Its striking shape gives a dramatic feel to the surrounding sea. The island looks just like a colossal hand had wrenched it up out of the waters. But the ferry can stop there thanks to the crude concrete pier. This island with its pier is called Mikura Island. The ferry doesn't stay long. But by mooring there it makes a connection with the land. Perhaps we should say that this connection is first passed through the concrete pier attached to the land. The mooring is a rope of tremendous size and toughness. In the sense that it is a thing for the purpose of connecting and binding, the goat is familiar with this rope. Because of the rope that kept him fastened to the slab of lumber. Because of the rope. The rope. The rope. And Tokyo. It's Tokyo. Then the ferry leaves Mikura. It continues heading north, then docks at Miyake Island. There's nothing much to say about that. Though it might be worth mentioning that the sun is beginning to sink. And it should certainly be said that when the moon comes out, the whole sea (that is, this one section of the Pacific Ocean) is bathed in light. It's a full moon. Full lunar phase. A sound rings out in the boat's hold, down on the level where all the shipping containers are neatly lined up. It reverberates like the tolling of a dull bell. No one notices it. But somewhere down there, from the inside of one of the containers – *Gong. Gong. Gong. Gong.* The sound is beaten out relentlessly. It's clearly the sound of a hand banging against something. No one notices because no one is on that level of the ship. It isn't time to unload cargo, so not a single member of the crew is stationed there.

The ferry maintains its course in a nearly straight line.

It makes a slight curve and continues on.

It's following the sea-lanes.

Eventually the ferry enters the Uraga Channel. It passes through the straits between the Bōsō and Miura Peninsulas, now cut off from the Pacific by Tokyo Bay. As it enters the harbour, crewmembers finally begin to appear in the hold. One or two, maybe three. And now, look. Or listen. Give this tale the respect it deserves in the mythology of tertiary Tokyo. *Gong. Gong. Gong. Gong. Gong.* Now the banging has been heard. It has been heard by humans (or rather by multiple eardrums). There's someone there. There's someone inside of one of the containers, banging desperately. It's forceful, insistent. The one or two, maybe three crewmembers – or maybe it was four or more who heard it – search for the source. They stop when they get to the special container for animal transport – *That's the one! That's where it's coming from!* It's still going. *Gong. Gong. Gong. Gong.* The door is bent outwards. There's a goat inside, one of the crewmembers thinks, so it must be ramming the door. The he-goat inside the container must be bashing his horns on the door over and over. But that's not what it sounds like. The impression of the sound (that is to say, its vibration) is undoubtedly that of a human hand knocking. But knocking fiercely. So the door is opened by those outside it.

Inside the container are all of the devices and equipment needed to transport a live goat.

The water has obviously been drunk. There are piles of droppings. The reek of urine is overpowering. Nearly all of the ashitaba has been eaten. And there is no goat. The lone male goat is missing, but there is a naked man.

He doesn't look like a castaway.

The crewmembers are astonished. They ask, 'Who are you?'

'I am a monster.'

The man looks to be in his mid-twenties, and is to all appearances Japanese. But 'Japanese,' as in a homogenous ethnicity made up of the Yamato race, is just a political fabrication. Saying that this man is to all appearances Japanese is a near-total surrender to this fantasy. The only objective fact that could possibly serve as proof of his being one of these illusory 'Japanese' is that he speaks in Japanese. When asked W-H-O A-R-E Y-O-U he answers I A-M A M-O-N-S-T-E-R. His answer is in Japanese. To these sailors, he might as well be declaring (or even affirming) I A-M A J-A-P-A-N-E-S-E M-O-N-S-T-E-R. *I am a Japanese monster.* In any case the man does not proclaim himself in the language of goats, or rather in the primordial language of instinctive communication that goats use, which is to say that he does not bleat. He is not listed on the ship's register. And the single male goat that was supposed to be inside the container in question is nowhere to be found – not in the hold or anywhere else on any of the other decks. Just to be sure the mess hall (or more specifically the galley) is searched, but there are no signs of any off-menu dishes prepared with goat meat. Time ticks on and before long the ferry reaches Takeshiba Pier in the innermost part of Tokyo Bay. It's moored according to the usual procedure. Once again the ferry is connected to the land, and this time the land is Takeshiba, which is to say, the Tokyo mainland. From the point of view of tertiary Tokyo, this mainland is where the primary and secondary Tokyos are. Right? If one accepts the existence of the tertiary, won't there also necessarily be a primary and a secondary? And also a difference between the visible and the hidden? So maybe there's a visible Tokyo and a hidden Tokyo. The mooring that connects the ferry to the Tokyo mainland is a rope of tremendous size and toughness. It is a thing for the purpose of connecting and binding two other separate things. Rope. Rope. Rope. And Tokyo. It's Tokyo. The monster has a burning desire to get off the boat, or to put it another way, he longs to be on solid ground. But those in charge of the ferry have to report to their supervisors, and they refuse to let the monster go on his way. This naked Japanese man (for this man of unknown origin has been deemed Japanese, or at least it is supposed that he is Japanese) cannot simply be released. This being the case, the monster naturally resorts to force. The two or three crewmembers – or maybe it was four, or even five or more who are investigating the situation – he kills them all. As a demonstration of his practical abilities, he slaughters them with his bare hands. He uses one hand to strangle, and both hands to wrench off heads. When he finally reaches land as he has so long wished to do, the monster is fully dressed in stolen clothing. He has shoes on too, though they don't quite fit. The sneaker on his left foot is too big, and the sandal on his right is too small. But the monster does not mind. He walks, trying to put distance between himself and the waterfront. Passing under the prefectural highway overpass and the elevated tracks of the loop line, he has no understanding of either the concept or the reality of what a loop line is. Not yet. After several minutes he comes to the JR Hamamatsu-chō Station. He learns how to buy a ticket from the machine by watching others do so. Then he takes the wallet out of his pocket, feeds some coins into the machine for a ticket, passes through the turnstile, and waits on the platform. Two JR trains approach the station, on the Keihin Tōhoku line and the Yamanote line. He boards the Yamanote train, which goes around the city in a loop – all the way around the urban centre of mainland Tokyo. The monster has a bodily sensation of travelling in a circle. Before long he makes use of his indispensable practical abilities. Seven or eight people, or maybe 80 people, or maybe 90 or more – he kills them all. He moves from carriage to carriage, killing as he goes, his act of slaughter on the Yamanote line orbiting the urban centre of mainland Tokyo. He rides the whole loop twice around. He wants to ride around again, but by now the authorities have been notified. The monster gets off at Shinjuku. With scrupulous attention to detail, he discards his right arm and attaches the right arm of his seventh victim; he switches out his left leg for the left leg of his tenth victim; he affixes to his face the nose from his 22nd victim; he takes the right ear of his 56th victim and the jaw of the 71st. He adds new parts and gets rid of the old ones. He has a brand new human appearance. Now, none of the various reports and eyewitness accounts of his actions will matter. Strangely enough, when the monster takes the brain from one of his victims (he can't recall which number victim it was) and uses it to replace his former brain, he has the definite sensation of having become someone else entirely. But something is bleating loudly – *mehhh*. His heart, which he has not yet replaced, bleats out a steady rhythm: *Mehhh. Mehhh. Mehhh.* All humans are created by something. The monster is an artificial human who has created himself. And then he flees the scene of the crime. He secures an ID card and a place to lay low. The police lead the exhaustive search for the whereabouts of the mass murderer who has suddenly appeared in the heart of urban Tokyo. The monster is forced to be extremely discreet in his movements. At a certain point he becomes acutely aware of mirrors. His consciousness is developed enough that he is now captivated by reflective surfaces. And also by fish tanks – but only those with saltwater in them, never fresh water. Why might this be? It's difficult to say. The monster prepares his meals with ingredients purchased at supermarkets, or convenience stores, or delicatessens. But four times a week without fail he must eat ashitaba. He cannot go without it. Which means that first he must obtain it. According to the explanation on the package in the vegetable aisle of one supermarket, ashitaba is a large perennial of the parsley family. The explanation goes on to say that ashitaba is in the *angelica* genus of the parsley family, a name that comes from the Latin *angelus,* which means angel. In the sixth month of his life in hiding, at one of the two supermarkets on the border between Shinjuku and Shibuya, the monster reaches for a package of ashitaba at the same moment that someone else is about to take it. For an instant, the monster's hand and that other person's hand touch. The monster looks up. The person is a woman. She looks to be in her mid-twenties. The monster realises that she has horns. They are short and white, pointing backwards in an elegant curve. Human beings cannot see these horns. The monster gives an experimental bleat: *Mehhh.* She answers, *Mehhh.* The monster smiles and thinks, *I'm saved at last.*

Picnic

Kaori Ekuni

Translated by Lydia Moëd

THE SMELL OF THE earth is strong. The fresh green grass grows longer day-by-day, in sharp points that know no fear – as befits something that has yet to be trodden down by anyone. It looks as if it's issuing a challenge to the world.

I stretch out my hand and touch the grass. It's coarse, yet soft. It has a sensual feel. On this clear, bright day, still chilly for spring, the grass feels damp even in the dry midday air. I move the palm of my hand, feeling the caress of the tips of the grass blades. It reminds me of putting my abacus on the floor as a child, and treading on it gently, spinning its beads around with the soles of my feet.

'Tickle'. As I skim my palm lightly over the grass, I think about the word in English. 'Tickle' – what would that word be, precisely, in Japanese? *Kusuguttai* would be close to it… but it's a little too rough to be called *kusuguttai*, this feeling. The grass under my hand doesn't know that if it had taken root somewhere else, only a few centimetres away, it would have been crushed. It would be under our red-white-and-blue striped picnic rug.

Kyoko and I each have a blanket over our laps; it's perhaps a little early in the year to be eating lunch outdoors. It's Sunday. But it's the second time this year we've come for a picnic in this park, five minutes' walk from our house. We'll probably do the same thing 20 more times until winter arrives and the grass becomes completely withered. We did that last year, and the year before. We have sandwiches, hard-boiled eggs, curried cauliflower, meatballs cooked in tomato sauce and more besides, packed together and arranged in different-sized airtight containers. We also have two vacuum flasks – one of coffee and one of sweet-corn soup.

'Is it okay?' Kyoko asks, as I put a piece of cauliflower in my mouth.

'Mm, it's good,' I say. She looks slightly relieved.

'I'm glad,' she says, putting her relief into words. You'd think it was the first time she'd ever given me food that she'd cooked for me herself. She can never get used to things.

'Lovely weather, isn't it?' she says, looking up at the sky. I gaze at her slender white throat as if I'm unused to looking at it. I see it as a weird, uncanny part of someone else's body. Surely Kyoko and I must seem like a happy couple.

We've been married for five years now. Because we didn't have much of a wedding, people I know – like my university friends and work colleagues, and the cousins I seldom see but feel close to anyway – often ask me what kind of person my wife is. They ask me how we fell in love, how we ended up getting engaged, that kind of thing. Every time I tell them it's a very boring story. I've never had anyone retract their questions after I've told them that, though.

This is our 'love story' – I'm not embarrassed to describe our journey from acquaintances to newlyweds in that way, though I'm not sure it's quite the right phrase. Anyway, here it is:

It began on New Year's Day when I was 26 years old. I went out to a nearby chain restaurant for lunch. There was a New Year's decoration hanging neatly on the door, and a special New Year's meal on the menu, too. The place was nearly empty. The only customers were a late-middle-aged man, a young woman, and me. I was intrigued by the woman, having lunch alone in a chain restaurant on New Year's Day, and when we'd finished eating I tried striking up a conversation with her. An iced tea arrived for her (she must have ordered it after her meal), and I ordered another coffee, separately. She didn't seem put off by this man suddenly appearing beside her and she didn't seem to be nervous or on edge, either – although having said that, nor did she seem particularly pleased. She chatted with me indifferently. That was Kyoko.

It's strange, thinking back on it now, but I knew I didn't make her nervous. I found that attractive. I asked her if I could call her and she readily gave me her number. She gave it so easily I wondered if it might be a fake number, but then when I called her about ten days later it was really her who picked up the phone.

Later, I found out that Kyoko still lived at home with her parents and her little sister. I had thought that her reason for having lunch in a chain restaurant on New Year's Day was the same as mine – that, like me, she was living alone, and, like me, she'd been feeling lonely and gone out to get some fresh air – but that wasn't it. She had 'just wanted to eat macaroni cheese'. She was two years younger than me and worked in a department store. Her father worked for a pharmaceutical company, her mother was a housewife, and her sister was at university.

Our relationship proceeded without a hitch. We ate together, watched films, went out for drives in a rented car. We kissed, went for walks, ate cake and ice cream and whatnot, went to hotels. We called one another, and exchanged emails, and after our dates I always walked her home. We attended a football match together and went on a trip to see the autumn leaves. When I took her back to my hometown, my parents really took a shine to her – even though they don't like me, their son, all that much. By contrast, her parents welcomed me lovingly – at least, it felt like they did.

After that we ended up here. Picnicking on a regular basis in a park five minutes' walk from our house.

'Be careful, won't you? It's hot,' Kyoko says, as I open the flask to pour some soup into a cup. A little way away from us some small children and their mothers are having an unseasonable picnic lunch, just like us. On the running track, on the other side of the grove of trees, walkers and joggers circle endlessly. On the other side of the track there's a gentle slope, overgrown with grass. Beyond the slope is wire netting and beyond the netting is a dual carriageway.

This park has several places better suited to a picnic than where we are now. On the grass that stretches as far as the eye can see, there's a gentle hill, and then there's the avenue of cherry trees which fills up with people when the blossom is out. But apparently, in Kyoko's opinion, going there would be 'embarrassing'.

Speaking of embarrassing things, the very act of having a picnic as a married couple surely qualifies as one. I find our picnic set pretty embarrassing as well: Kyoko went to a shop that sold high-end Western consumer goods – Williams-Sonoma cookware and Catherine Memmi furnishings and I-don't-know-what-else – and bought a full matching picnic set including a rug, a picnic basket and a top-of-the-range vacuum flask.

When I mention that picnicking is my wife's hobby and that she and I often go for a picnic – every week, weather permitting – most people are surprised. When they get over their surprise they smile at me oddly and say that it's great, or that they're envious or something. If they really feel like that they should try it themselves.

We didn't develop our picnicking habit until we got married. Kyoko herself hadn't ever been for a picnic before, whether with family or with friends or boyfriends. She started all of a sudden. It began with a walk on one of our days off.

'Let's go for a walk!' she said. 'Do you want to have lunch out?'

I thought she was suggesting going to a restaurant but that wasn't it – she said she simply wanted to eat outdoors.

And so we would walk, and we would buy bread and rice balls, bento boxes and yakisoba, and we would sit on park benches, on the edges of fountains, on deserted stone steps, or anywhere else we could sit, and we'd eat, and then we'd go home. Every week. Of course I got fed up and told Kyoko that I'd like to eat something she'd cooked occasionally. She looked sad.

That's when she started packing picnics. Because 'this way we can eat home-made food!' It was in mid-summer. The grass smelled fragrant, a breeze swayed the branches, and leaf-dappled sunlight spilled down on us. Uninhibited people, near-naked, tanned their skin in the sun. The air was sweet as nectar – so much so that I almost expected to see bees everywhere. As for my wife, she was lovely in every way. I was struck by her subtle allure and I felt fresh pleasure at the thought that someone so lovely was also equipped with the domestic skill to produce this meal, packed in airtight containers.

I moved closer and buried my nose in her hair, pressed my lips to her neck. I laid my head on her outstretched legs and dozed there from time to time. She made a contented sound, a little chuckle in her throat. She combed her fingers gently through my hair.

We are happy, I thought. I was suddenly enraptured by the soporific scent of summer and the bright open air, Kyoko's cool fingers, the lively atmosphere around us, a full stomach. The words – 'We are happy' – came into my mouth and I just said them. After a little while I heard her say 'That's good', in a soft, smiling voice. *That's good.* Isn't that a strange answer?

It was about then that I began to think that this woman, Kyoko, was kind of like a witch.

Even before that I had noticed several things about her that I found eccentric but I could only base that observation on my limited experience of other women I have known, so I just thought she was a bit of a character. For example, no matter how hard she tried, she could never remember my name. She sometimes correctly called me Hiroyuki but she spoke as if lacking confidence, with a questioning tone to her voice. Other times she called me Yukihiro (again with a slight questioning tone). Or she'd say, 'Hiroyuki – I mean Yukihiro,' or, 'It was Yukihiro, wasn't it?' or she'd falter: 'Erm… I'm sorry…'. I thought it was funny. I corrected her to begin with, but in the end it got ridiculous. I don't believe she meant any harm by it. Instead, it gave me a strange kind of pleasure to say to her generously, 'You can call me whatever you like.'

I'd bet money that, even now, she doesn't quite remember my name. Because she's taken to calling me 'dearest' all the time, like couples did in the old days. Dearest, look at this. Dearest, try this. Dearest. Things like my name have no meaning for Kyoko.

Here's another example. Kyoko has never whispered sweet nothings to me. When I say that kind of thing to her she laughs quietly in the usual pleased-sounding way and replies, 'I'm glad'. That's it. She never says 'I want you too' or anything like that. It's particularly striking when we're in bed together. We spend the time doing everything I want to do. She spreads her slim white legs and leans back. Or she straddles me, tossing her hair. When she takes me in her mouth, or I bury my face in her pussy, or I suck her toes one by one, she doesn't seem to dislike it. I can be fierce, aching, rough. I try not to be rough – I get closer and closer. I thrust into her, fall upon her, hold on, withdraw, thrust again, thrust again. At last, after a breathless moment, I am released with a gasp.

'That was amazing,' I say, panting. Even then, she looks at me with a mystified expression and says, 'I'm glad to hear it,' or, 'oh right?'

These kinds of thing are trivial – they *tickle* like prickly grass. Serious as a hangnail.

Today's sandwiches are roast ham. Thick, satisfying slices, smothered with butter and mustard. We polish them off and I sip some coffee.

'Look,' Kyoko says. 'A cat.'

A black cat is traversing a thicket of shrubs. Perhaps it's because I've just eaten, or perhaps it's because of the afternoon sun, but I feel much warmer now than I did when we arrived. I stretch and put the lap blanket aside. I fall back and lie face-up, the upper half of my body stretching beyond the picnic rug, touching the ground directly. The cool scent of earth. Blue sky. I close my eyes and try to sense the thin sunlight through my eyelids. I can feel the breeze fluttering my eyelashes.

'That's a weird place to lie,' Kyoko says. 'Get up. You can nap after lunch.'

I once asked Kyoko why she liked picnics so much. It was after we'd picnicked four or five times since that first day at the height of summer.

'Because…' Kyoko said. 'Because, when I look at you outside, I can see you clearly. I can see the size of you, the shape of your hands, your voice, your presence.'

'You can see my presence?'

'Of course,' she said, nodding. 'Every creature asserts its existence through its presence first of all, right? And besides,' she continued, smiling, 'when you have a picnic, you feel like you're not all alone.'

I remember I stopped still. I was holding the basket, and had the picnic rug under one arm.

'*Are* you all alone?' I asked, and Kyoko looked at me, surprised.

'Don't say silly things,' she said, and giggled. 'Only a barefaced idiot would say something like that.'

'Well, that's me,' I replied. She gave me an unusually piercing look. 'Aren't you able to see me inside the house?'

'I can see you. But not well,' was the reply.

'What do you mean by "not well"?' I asked, to show that

I could be sensible too, when I felt like it. Kyoko took a breath and made a long, thin, resigned-sounding noise, like a whistle.

'Not as you should be,' she confessed. She sounded apologetic but there was a vivid light in her eyes.

'Not as I should be. I see,' I said with a wry smile, though naturally I was deeply upset.

Pathological honesty.

I don't know whether this is just a character trait of Kyoko's or whether it's something all women have in common (it makes me feel like a wounded animal caught in a trap). But Kyoko, at least, definitely has it. I think it's this trait that makes witches witches – people who have it aren't really people at all. Pathological honesty. I hate that trait from the bottom of my heart.

I sit up and take another sandwich. At the bottom of the slope, on the footpath beside the road, I can see a child riding a tricycle. An old woman, probably the child's grandmother, is walking slowly alongside. From our point of view they seem to travel tremendously slowly from left to right. In the bushes, where the black cat was earlier, two glossy little dark-brown birds are hopping about, pecking at something on the ground – or perhaps at the ground itself.

Kyoko, who has just finished eating, returns to the paperback on her lap. Her downcast eyelashes are thin. Her flat nose and smooth cheeks are as white as pounded rice.

No doubt the thing she has found most surprising about married life is the fact that my existence is unpleasant and incomprehensible to her. I am a contaminant – I don't belong indoors. I think she drags me outside like this to let the sun fall on me and the wind blow through me, to air me out like a futon.

'Thanks for lunch,' I say. Kyoko raises her head from her book. Her defenceless lips stick out plumply. I crawl forwards on the rug until I reach those lips. The plastic containers are scattered around, so I take care where I place my hands. Kyoko gives a start but straight away she dutifully accepts my lips. She puts one hand behind her so as not to fall, and holds the back of my head with the other.

'Look closely,' I whisper. I lean over Kyoko, contaminating her with my size, the shape of my hands, my voice, my presence, and I bite her lip and pull.

To me it's Kyoko who is a contaminant. Just like the little brown birds, and the cat that crossed the shrubbery, and the child on the tricycle.

I put my hand under the blanket and feel Kyoko flinch. The shape of her legs, dressed simply in blue jeans. I see only fear in her eyes now.

I smile. I take my hand off her jeans and instead gradually let my body drop, crushing Kyoko with my weight. Our cheeks rub together and the tip of my nose touches the grass.

'You're heavy!' Kyoko says. I ignore her, smell the scent of the damp earth and take a bite of the tickly grass. The green taste of the grass is mingled with the taste of earth.

A muffled laugh. Underneath me, Kyoko's chest heaves. 'What are you doing? You're heavy.'

I move reluctantly aside and we lie next to each other, stretched out face-up. The sun is in our eyes.

'The sun's in my eyes,' I say.

Kyoko says the same thing.

'And my neck's cold. The grass is scritchy.'

I lift my arm and put it on my face, covering my eyes. The sunbeams are thwarted. I can hear somebody laughing, far away. I can hear somebody else doing drum practice. I know that next to me Kyoko is sitting up and has started putting away the picnic things. I stay put, rather than helping her. The wind, the rustling leaves, the sound of the drums.

A diffident voice floats down from somewhere above my head. 'Get up, dearest,' it says. But I hear it far away, as if the words are addressed to somebody else. Then they are sucked up into the empty sky. She probably spoke those words facing the sky – fearlessly, eccentrically.

My eyelids don't move. Not a twitch

A House for Two

Mitsuyo Kakuta

Translated by Hart Larrabee

I ENJOY SHOPPING. WHENEVER I shop, I get the feeling that good things are going to happen, especially if I've bought clothing or lingerie. I skip down the steps to the subway and reach the platform just as the red train is rolling into the station. This seems like one of the good things – proof that they're already starting to happen.

Standing by the door of the train, it strikes me that this is the sort of thing a man would never understand. Take Haraguchi, for example. I'm pretty sure he wouldn't understand. And since he's the only man I know very well, as far as I'm concerned he represents all the men in the whole world. Well, at least all the Japanese men.

A lot of passengers get off at Shinjuku, leaving the carriage mostly empty. I sit at the end of a centre-facing bench seat, take the almost weightless paper bag I've been holding in my hand, and place it gently on my lap. I lean forward and breathe in deeply through my nose. Although it's impossible, I'm certain I catch a hint of the sweet smell of flowers.

I often come across things I think men would never understand. Indeed, I'm almost positive no man could ever understand most of the things I feel. Not just the good things that happen after shopping, but also my insistence that one should work back from dessert when selecting among the options for a full-course meal, or the enormous difference between a gift box with a ribbon and one without, or the fragrant smell of a brand new book, or the existence of a colour that is definitely not cream and could only possibly be described as eggshell. Thinking how a man would never be able to understand such things reminds me that I would never be able to live with one. It's a refreshing thought.

Not every woman wants to pair up with a man. Not every woman who is single is looking for love. Not when there is so much in life that is richer and more beautiful.

The train comes to a stop. I get off with a few others and board the carriage waiting on the other side of the platform. A couple of minutes later, we move off into the darkness.

★

Heading through the turnstiles and back to the surface, I look up the stairwell and see a white rectangle – a glowing portal of light, taller than it is wide. It fades as I climb the steps and the scenery comes into view.

I cross at the lights and follow the pavement past a handful of shops on that side of the street. The sky is clear and the air comfortably warm. There aren't many pedestrians on a weekday. My mood picks up as I walk. I stop in at a new pastry shop then continue home with a box of cakes in my right hand and the paper bag in my left. The shops come to an end, followed by rows of apartments and private homes.

My house is about a 20-minute walk from the station. The cherry tree is completely bare of blossoms now, its branches as dense with leafy greenery as those of the silverberry and the barren plum. I pass beneath the gate and over the flagstones, slide open the front door, and call out to my mother.

'Nobu-chan, I got us some cake!'

'Oh, really?' Her voice comes drifting down the hall. 'From where?'

'You know that fancy new place that opened up in the shopping arcade? From there.' I remove my shoes and arrange them neatly in the entryway before proceeding into the house. Mother is ironing in the living room.

'Ooh, I'd been thinking I might buy something there myself. I wonder if it's any good?' She smiles. 'I'll put some tea on.'

'No, no,' I say, 'I'll do it,' raising a hand to stop her from getting up as I head toward the kitchen on the far side of the living room. I fill the kettle with water, twist the knob on the gas stove, and take the teapot down from the cupboard.

Mother comes in and opens the box. 'Well, don't these look lovely?'

'Nobu-chan, you can pick whichever one you want.'

'That's all right, Ku-chan. You choose first.'

'Okay. I'll have the tart. Why don't we each eat one now and save the other two for after dinner?'

'Good idea. I'll take the white one, then. I wonder what is it? Cheesecake, maybe?'

I ready our tea as we speak, place everything on a tray, and carry it into the living room. The ironing is all done, with the clothes on their hangers and the iron standing upright on the ironing board.

'Ku-chan,' Mother says from the kitchen. 'Don't touch the iron. It's still hot.' Ever since I was a little girl, Mother's been telling me not to touch the iron because it's still hot. She still thinks of me as a child, as if I haven't grown at all since I was about four years old.

Sitting next to me on the sofa, Mother asks, 'When will the grocery delivery arrive?'

'It should be here tomorrow.'

'Thanks. That's such a big help. Rice and the like are so heavy I just can't carry them myself anymore. Ooh, this cake is delicious. That new shop's a real winner.'

'I think so, too. Better than I expected. While I was out I also picked up some lingerie. Guess what? It's Eres.'

'It's what?'

'Eres. It's a French brand. It's expensive, but it's *really* lovely.'

'Well, then, let's have a look.'

'Okay. In a bit.'

'Is lingerie the only thing you shopped for?'

'Let's see. After finishing up at the food market in the basement I did go to the fourth floor to look at women's wear, but there was nothing special.'

'Well, it *is* between seasons. Not the best time for buying clothes.'

The conversation comes to a halt. Mother gets up and flips the switch on the television, immediately flooding the living room with noise. One of the daytime variety shows is running a feature on health. The commentators in the studio are shrieking excitedly while engaged in some bizarre form of exercise. I finish my cake, then pick up the paper bag at my feet and pull it near. I gently draw out the tissue-wrapped package within and proceed to open it carefully.

'This is it,' I say. '*This* is Eres.' Mother shifts her gaze from the television to the lingerie spread out on my lap.

'My, that's rather....' She stops, then asks, 'How much was it?'

'The bra was 28,000 yen, the knickers 12,000.'

'That's quite pricey.'

'Yes, well, they're French.'

'Try them on.'

'Okay. I think I will.'

I carry the lingerie down the hallway to the bath. I take off my clothes in the changing room, remove my underwear, and put on my brand new lingerie. I like the way it feels as it glides on.

If I were to tell my girlfriends – or even Mon-chan – that I modelled my underwear in front of my mother they would probably look at me funny. But I show Mother everything I buy. I slip on new shoes for her to see, and new dresses, so of course I show her new underwear, too. My sister Mon-chan is three years younger than me. Despite being born and raised by the same mother in this very same house, around the time she hit puberty she began concealing everything she bought. She took everything to her room in secret: clothes, shoes, bags, even magazines. As if Mother wouldn't find out eventually. Mon-chan always used to say she couldn't understand me, but I was never able to figure out what she was thinking, either.

'Well?' comes Mother's voice from outside the changing room. 'How are they?'

'Ta-dah!' I say as I throw open the door.

'Well, now that they're on, they look perfectly wonderful. If a bit swimsuity.'

'And worth the price, too. Look how high my breasts are now.'

'You do have an impressive physique,' Mother smiles as she heads back to the living room. I quickly put my clothes back on and check the position of my breasts in the mirror. They're definitely higher.

'Why don't I do the food shopping, today?' I ask Mother as she clears the cake plates.

'Well, in that case, let's go together. I was thinking four o'clock or so, but it's such a nice day we could head out a bit earlier.'

'Great idea,' I say as I sit down on the sofa in the living room. 'The weather's just right for a walk. It'll feel good.' On television, the exercise segment has ended and the commentators who were so giddy a short while ago are now talking in all seriousness about a murder.

★

Mon-chan left home at the age of twenty, and made quite a scene on her way out. Mother said she couldn't understand why Mon-chan had to go off and live on her own when she had a perfectly good house in the city from which to commute to university – and what would people think? Aside from the last part, I did feel Mother had a point. But Mon-chan became furious. 'How many times do I have to tell you: that's not the issue. Do I have to spell it out for you? All right, I'll say it. I… I hate this house and I hate you, too! I understand why Dad left. He must have hated it here!' Mon-chan could just as well have spoken normally but was literally screaming through her tears.

Our father left home for another woman when I was in high school and Mon-chan was in junior high. Mother never told us where he went or who the other woman was. One day I came home from school and found Mother crouching in the garden. The trembling of her rounded back made me think at first that she must be crying, but when I shifted position to look at her hands I could see this wasn't the case at all. She was digging at the dirt with a shovel like a child's toy, the hands that gripped it plunging again and again into the earth. I didn't know what she was doing, but I was pretty sure I'd seen something I shouldn't have. I knew it would be best to slip into the house and pretend I hadn't seen anything, but I was rooted to the spot. Mother turned around and noticed me. Making no effort to hide her soiled hands, she smiled wanly and said, 'What would you like for dinner tonight?'

Mon-chan took a job at a health foods company after getting out of university, married a man from the same organisation when she was 27, and now has two children. She still seems to hate this house and rarely comes to visit. Mother, who Mon-chan had flatly declared she hated, never visits Mon-chan, either.

'I just don't know how to deal with that girl,' Mother once said. 'Sometimes I can't even believe she's my own flesh and blood. Like when she left home. What was *that* all about? All that howling and crying. What had I ever done to her?'

I suppose Mother just couldn't forgive her for bringing

Father into it. Even now, fifteen years later, I still don't think she can. Sometimes I wonder if she might hate Mon-chan just like she hates Father. That would explain why she makes no effort to see Mon-chan's children.

Since I quit my job I've been visiting Mon-chan at her home once every three or four months. As the oldest daughter I feel a responsibility not to leave the rift between my mother and my younger sister completely unbridged. Mon-chan still works for the same company she always has, so I visit in the evening or on weekends. She lives in Chiba prefecture, in Motoyawata, in a condominium purchased with a 35-year mortgage.

I once asked Mon-chan what it was that she had hated about our house and about Nobu-chan. I think this was when she was pregnant with her first child. It was a weekday, so she must have been on maternity leave.

'I suppose just that she was so controlling,' Mon-chan replied as she prepared dinner. 'In junior high, I realised she was going into my room without permission while I was at school. She checked everything: letters, my diary, even things I had scribbled in my textbooks. I very clearly asked her to stop, but she just insisted she'd done nothing of the sort. And that's not all. She wouldn't tell me when I had telephone calls from boys, and always tried to decide what I should do with my life. And of course there's the whole thing with Dad. If she wants to hate him, that's her business, but don't you remember how she tried to make us hate him, too? The fact that we were able to carry on with our lives, just as we had before, without her having to work, means he must have been providing support. He was always a good father to me, and I'm grateful to him for that. I wanted to tell him I'd been accepted to my first-choice college, and do you know what she said? "I'm sure he's forgotten all about you. After all, he abandoned you, remember?" I thought I'd go crazy if I had to stay there any longer, so for the first two years of college I barely went to class and spent all my time doing part-time jobs to save money.' Mon-chan shot me a look mixed with condescension and added, 'Not that I really expect you to know what I mean.'

It was all I could do to keep from bursting out laughing. I'd known since elementary school that our mother rummaged through our rooms while we were out. And I understood the reason why: because we hid things. So I cleared my room of secrets. I simply left my letters and my diary spread open on my desk. I did the same with the tests I failed and my address book. I showed Mother everything I bought. It was a mystery to me how Mon-chan could have failed for nearly a decade to grasp the simple logic that only what is hidden can be exposed. As for the telephone calls from boys and the issue of where to go to university, I'd have to say Mon-chan was just unlucky. Having gone directly from the girls' high school that Mother recommended into a women's college, I never had to worry about calls from boys, and we never argued about what I'd do after graduation. Surely there must have been some other way Mon-chan could have handled things. And as far as that business with our father is concerned, objectively speaking what Mother had said was correct: we had been abandoned. It isn't as if he would have congratulated Mon-chan even if she had called to tell him she'd got into university. I'm sure Mother simply spoke firmly because she didn't want her to get hurt. It all came down to the fact that Mon-chan was still a child. I found this little sister of mine, with the smug look in her eyes, unbearably funny.

Mon-chan gave birth to a daughter when she was 29 and a son when she was 31. The girl is now six and the boy turns four this year. Mon-chan has been sending them to nursery school since they were babies and continues to work. She has a habit of saying, 'I'm not going to end up like Mum.' And indeed, her house is the exact opposite of ours. It's always messy and unclean, with ready-meals or take-aways on the table. Her husband does the dishes and folds the laundry without complaint. Her children are like wild animals. Mon-chan doesn't scold them even when they eat standing up or when they scuffle and fight, and she never dresses Rikuko in pink or makes Kaito study English.

And after all that...? On the way home I had to suppress the urge to laugh. After all that, Mon-chan still measured herself against our mother, didn't she? She may have thought she had escaped from Mother and the house, but she was still shackled to both. Mon-chan really was still just a child.

★

'Nobu-chan,' I say to my mother at breakfast. 'I won't need lunch today.'

She cocks one eyebrow and says, 'Nikawa?' Nikawa is the only former classmate I still keep in touch with. After getting divorced two years ago, she's living with her parents now, too.

'No. Haraguchi,' I answer. Mother's nostrils flare momentarily.

'Oh, him,' she says, spreading butter on her toast. 'Where are you meeting?'

'Near his office. He says there's a little restaurant there with fantastic cutlets.'

'Oh, you're having pork for lunch, then? In that case, why don't we have sashimi for dinner? Something light.'

'If the cutlet place is as good as he says, we'll have to go together sometime soon.'

'All right,' Mother smiles. 'But you'll have to grade it strictly. You just never know with that Haraguchi.' She continues smiling as she removes the crust cleanly from her toast. 'I mean, he says everything he eats is delicious. Remember that time when Chiyo Sushi was closed and we had to go to a place we'd never tried before and it was so awful it was barely edible but Haraguchi kept going on and on about how delicious it was? I wondered if perhaps he'd never eaten sushi before.'

'You remember how big he is, don't you? I think his nerves just don't reach all the way to the surface. It's the best his tongue can do to distinguish between what's food and what's not. And anything he recognises as food is automatically delicious.'

'Well,' Mother smiled again.

Haraguchi was a colleague at the first company I worked for. I later took jobs at a number of other places, and now, of course, I just live at home without working at all, but Haraguchi stayed put. When I was 23, he told me he loved me. I reported this to Mother and she told me to bring him to the house. We never did become lovers but have always remained friends. I even took my mother to his wedding.

'You don't have something going on with Haraguchi, do you?' asks Mother, eating her now crust-free toast with a topping of omelette.

'Of course not! Not when he'll be paying child support for the next 20 years.' Haraguchi had divorced when he was 30. Apparently, the agreement with his ex-wife committed him to pay child support until retirement.

'Well, I suppose you're right. But you can't stay here forever. Instead of spending time with Haraguchi you really ought to be looking for someone good.'

'Oh, all right,' I answer with a playful roll of my eyes and leave the dining room. I hear Mother's voice call after me: 'Sweep up out by the gate, would you?'

I answer, 'Oh, all right' one more time and step outside.

⋆

It was last year, after I'd quit my job, when Mon-chan asked, 'Don't you get scared?' After dinner with her feral children and her husband who chews with his mouth open, she had offered to see me to the station, something she did only rarely.

At first, when she said, 'Don't you get scared?' I thought it was just more of her sarcasm and irony, but she looked perfectly serious and seemed genuinely concerned for me.

When I asked, 'Of what?' she said, 'It just looks like *that woman* is taking over your life.' I was a bit put off by the way she referred to Mother but she carried on, looking perfectly serious. 'At this rate you'll never get out,' she said. 'You're always with her. Your whole world is just the two of you. That's all fine and good while she's alive, but what will you do when she dies? You'll be all alone.' As we walked down the darkened street I didn't answer right away, so Mon-chan added, 'I can't shake the feeling that she's using you as a tool to get revenge.'

'On who? On Dad?'

'No. On herself. She can't stand the thought that you might end up happier than she did. Keeping you all alone is her way of punishing herself.'

'That doesn't make any sense,' I said with a laugh. And in fact, I really didn't understand what she meant. Why would Mother feel she had to get revenge on herself? Why would she need to keep me all alone? 'What I mean is,' I said, 'I've made all of my own choices.' *Not like you*, I added in my heart. *Not like you and the way you're chained to Mother by always doing the opposite of what she would want.*

'Well, if that's the case,' Mon-chan said with an air of resignation, 'then I guess that's all right.' She kept waving for a long time after we parted at the turnstiles. Every time I turned around to look back she was still there, waving to me.

★

Yoshida from two doors up the street walks past wearing a tracksuit. 'Good morning,' he says with a smile, wiping his brow with a towel. Still gripping the handle of the broom, I smile back and nod in greeting. Yoshida took up jogging in April. Apparently he always runs down to Chuo Park, does a lap of the perimeter, and then comes back. When he passes our house the neighbour's dog Becky invariably barks at him. 'Easy there, girl,' he says nervously, then looks back at me with a smile and hurries on toward the gate of his own house.

There's no way anything is going to happen with Haraguchi, but I do slip into the new Eres lingerie I bought a few days ago. I change into the blouse Mother ironed for me and put on a skirt I bought in early spring, but then I realise this might give Mother ideas so I pull on a pair of black slacks instead. I poke my head into the living room to say goodbye. Mother looks up from the lacework she's doing in front of the television, hands me a note and says, 'Could you pick up a few dinner groceries on your way home?' I take the list and leave the house. It's another fine day. The breeze is gentle and my underwear is brand new. On the upper floor of an apartment building, carp streamers[2] someone has forgotten to take down flutter merrily in the wind.

★

I nearly got married once. I was 29. Almost all of my friends had married and I was feeling impatient. I was convinced I had to get married at all costs before I turned 30. I signed up with a matchmaking service and met a number of men, including one I thought might be alright to marry. His name was Moto Akasaka. He was 31, worked at a trading company, and was the second son of a family of sake brewers in Saitama prefecture. I don't know that you would call it love, but the time I spent with Moto always felt fluffy somehow. The asphalt and the hanging straps on the trains and the doors and the tables – everything I came into contact with seemed soft and diaphanous. We went to movies and took drives and had meals together. After six months, he asked me to marry him. When I returned home and told Mother she was so happy she cried, so I telephoned Moto and relayed my acceptance.

---

2. Also known as 'Koinobori'; carp-shaped wind socks traditionally flown to celebrate May 5th, Children's Day, a national holiday.

It must have started with the ring or the dinner, although at this point I can't remember clearly which. Mother's criticism of the engagement ring Moto gave me and of our dinner out with his parents was restrained but persistent. The ring was a decorated band, which Mother said showed a 'lack of common sense.' She frowned when she saw it and said, 'Engagement rings are to be diamond solitaires. That looks like it was bought at some street fair.' Unexpectedly, she then walked the department stores until she found the very same ring and checked its price. 'What kind of man gives an engagement ring that costs only fifty thousand yen? Ku-chan,' she said as she began to cry, 'he's making a fool of you.' When I comforted her and said I didn't think it was cause for tears, she said, 'What kind of mother sits calmly by as her daughter is humiliated like this?' and buried her face in her hands.

The dinner out was a disaster, too. Whether by virtue of their profession or something in their blood, the members of Moto's family were all heavy drinkers. His father and mother, and older brother and sister-in-law, too, all consumed a shocking amount of alcohol. All smiles, they even tried to compel us to keep pace with them. When I only sipped at the glasses they filled, Moto's father started giving me a hard time, asking how I was going to manage as a brewer's wife if I couldn't drink. I knew immediately that Mother was displeased. She sat sullenly and silently without touching either food or drink. Then Moto's father caught his leg on the table as he stood to go to the bathroom, knocking all the sake bottles that had been set on its corner to the floor and spilling their contents.

'We did not,' Mother said in a voice that oozed annoyance, 'come here to carouse.'

Then Moto's father said, 'What are you getting all high and mighty about?' and there was a brief argument.

The grilled course had only just been served but Mother said, 'Let's go,' took my hand, and pulled me from the room. Ignoring Moto's timorous efforts to follow after and prevent us from leaving, she left the restaurant and, once out on the street, raised a hand to flag a cab.

In the taxi Mother said, 'Are you sure that family's really right for you?' I was relieved to hear her speak in such a gentle voice despite her obvious displeasure. 'I mean, they have such dreadful manners; are you really content to be called a "brewer's wife."'

'But,' I said. 'Moto lives on his own, and he's the second son, and we've already started to make all sorts of decisions. It's too late to just call things off now.' Intending to be funny I said, 'I mean, it isn't as if his father is going to come over every night and pour me drinks.' I laughed, but Mother didn't even smile. In the gloomy taxi I lowered my head and quietly said, 'I'm sorry.'

'It's all because your father left us,' Mother said. 'To think that as an only parent, marrying you into a family like that is the best I can manage.'

It isn't as if I took everything Mother said at face value. I didn't think the 50,000 yen engagement ring was humiliating, and I certainly didn't think having only one parent had any bearing at all on my marriage to Moto. Still, the whole episode did become an occasion for self-reflection. Why was I so set on marrying Moto? Why did I even want to get married at all? Was it really right to make such an important life decision with the mind-set of a schoolgirl who longs for the same sort of mechanical pencil everyone else has?

Ultimately, I decided to call off the marriage. The fluffiness I had felt had been neither love nor affection. To spend my life with a man I didn't love because of mere impatience was just being irresponsible towards myself. Plans for the ceremony had only gone as far as touring potential venues, and although Moto's boss had agreed to serve as our go-between, surely amends could be made somehow. If I was going to back out, this was the time. This was the time to take control of my own life. I made my decision and told Mother

I was calling off the wedding.

I thought she would be happy. I thought she would be profoundly relieved to hear that her daughter would no longer be marrying into a family with dreadful manners that treated her like a fool. Mother, however, strenuously objected: 'Marriage is where a woman finds true happiness, and if you're going to have children it's better to start earlier. What will people think? His parents are a bit much, but it isn't as if you'll be moving in with them and taking over the family business. Think this over carefully. Please, think it over just one more time.'

Strangely, though, the more Mother pushed the idea of going ahead with the marriage, the more firmly resolved I became to call it off. My feelings had cooled completely, so much so that I wondered if I had been under some kind of hypnosis when I wanted to marry Moto. When she realised that no amount of persuasion would change my mind, Mother gave up. It was she who contacted Moto and his family to relay the news and to apologise.

When I told Mon-chan what had happened, she said, 'You know, your whole life is being ruined.'

'Well,' I said. 'I'm grateful, actually, not to be marrying someone I don't love.' Mon-chan looked at me as if she had seen something unsettling, started to speak, and then stopped. The following year Mon-chan got married so suddenly that, had she been a celebrity, it would surely have been called a 'whirlwind romance', which made me realise I kind of knew what she'd started to say but didn't. She probably wanted to say that *she* wasn't going to end up like me.

For some time after that Mother often teased: 'I wonder what that brewer's boy is up to. He seemed kind of helpless, but probably wasn't the sort to go having affairs with other women. What a wasted opportunity, Ku-chan. Wherever did you get such a stubborn streak?'

★

Waiting for the light to change at the crossing on the way to the station, I mull over Mother's contradictions. On the one hand, she reproaches me for wanting to marry into 'a family like that'; on the other, she needles me about what a missed opportunity it was. She pokes fun at Haraguchi even as she hints I ought to get something going with him. She tells me to find someone good, but if I did she would probably just rattle off his bad points.

The light turns green and I suddenly remember what Mon-chan said as we were walking that night last year, the part about Mother using me as a tool for revenge.

Oh, so that's it. Now I see. I finally understand what Mon-chan was trying to say, and the puzzle of all Mother's contradictions is solved. She wants me to be happy, and at the same time doesn't want me to be happy. It must have to do with her feelings about her own past. She wants to believe she was happy, but realises she cannot. And how could she? But what Mon-chan had said wasn't exactly correct. Mother isn't using me as a tool of revenge; Mother thinks of me as herself, a self who should be *right there*, all alone, digging away at the dirt.

I'm sure Mon-chan would never understand, but even now I remain grateful for all that Mother has done. I'm grateful that, in researching the price of the ring, and writing off Moto's family as vulgar, she gave me the opportunity to take a good hard look at my life.

★

The cutlet place Haraguchi takes me to seems to be very popular; by the time we arrive, there's already a line. We take our place at the end and catch up on each other's latest.

'Bought a condo, you know,' Haraguchi says suddenly.

'Really? I thought you were still paying child support?'

'It's a *really* long-term loan.'

'How come, all of the sudden?'

'I've been thinking seriously about finding a life partner.' He looks so earnest I nearly laugh. 'No, really, I mean it,' he says, looking at me closely.

'Wait, you decide to look for a life partner and the first thing you do, even before going to mixers or trying to set up an arranged marriage, is buy a condo?

'Well, I figure having a house sweetens the deal.'

'Ah, I see. You come with perks.'

The door slides open. Two men in business shirts step out and two women who look like office girls step in.

'How about you?' Haraguchi asks. 'You aren't looking for work? Surely your mother must be better by now.'

'Oh, I'll start looking again soon,' I say, even though it has already been about a year. I had told Haraguchi I was quitting my last job because Mother was ill and I needed to care for her. That had been a lie, of course. Although she turned 70 last year, Mother has not so much as caught a cold in the last decade. The real reason was that it just became too stressful to have to adjust my values to those of the other people at the office. I simply couldn't stand having people pry into my background as a 38-year-old woman with no boyfriend who lives alone with her mother – all their offering of advice and worrying on my behalf. During my second year at the company, I noticed I had a bald spot about the size of a one yen coin. That's what led me to quit. I haven't told Mother about the bald spot. I suppose it's my first secret.

'So, you've retired, then?'

'Well, things *are* nice and relaxed. And I don't have to worry what other people think. Why are you so anxious to get remarried, anyway? Why not just enjoy having your new condo all to yourself?'

'What a lonely thing to say.'

The door slides open again. This time a group of garishly dressed middle-aged women filter out. The turnover is surprisingly quick.

'Lonely?'

'Sometimes I think maybe you just don't even know how to feel lonely,' Haraguchi says, gazing at me intently. The man and woman ahead of us in the queue enter the restaurant. Finally, it's our turn next. The aroma of cooking oil wafts out into the street.

'Well, who needs to feel lonely? Better not to, I think. It keeps me out of needless trouble.'

'When your mother's gone, though, I think maybe you'll realise what lonely is.'

'We'll see,' I say, then quickly correct myself: 'I'm sure you're right.' For a moment, I think I won't feel the least bit lonely when Mother dies. Actually, not so much *think* as *know*. This kind of gives me the chills.

'You're a strong one,' says Haraguchi, in a voice that betrays a sense of irritation at odds with his words. I can't decide whether he's just annoyed about the long wait or about a certain insensitivity he sees in me.

The office girl types come out, their lips glistening. We're called in and shown to the counter. The place is filled with the smell of oil and a lively clamour rises from the packed tables. Haraguchi orders us two pork roast cutlets. Cups of tea arrive. I look around. The walls are almost completely covered with faded posters, the screen of the television mounted near the ceiling has corners dark with grime, and ceramic tanuki figurines of all sizes are on display everywhere. *Definitely a failing grade*, I think to myself. *Mother wouldn't like it here.*

The pork cutlets we've brought are huge and as thick as steaks. I apply a liberal dose of mustard and bring a bite to my mouth; the breading is crunchy and fragrant and the meat surprisingly tender.

'It's delicious,' I say to Haraguchi at my side.

'Isn't it?' he answers proudly. 'You need to get out more instead of spending so much time at home. The world is full of delicious things, you know.' While trying hard to sound persuasive, Haraguchi still manages to gobble down a piece of pork cutlet and shovel in a mouthful of rice.

'Eating good food,' I say, 'makes me feel as if all is right with the world.

'And how.' Haraguchi nods enthusiastically, even though he can hardly have understood what I meant.

Whenever we have lunch together we always go out for coffee afterwards, but after standing in line for cutlets we're running late. 'I'm sorry to invite you out and not have time for coffee,' Haraguchi says as he walks me to the station.

Walking at his side, I think back on how I myself once commuted to this neighbourhood. I was in my early twenties. I wore suits Mother had helped me pick out. Everything in the world seemed fresh and new and even the crowded trains and the parade of business people on the street seemed agreeable. I always enjoyed looking at the menus out in front of the restaurants and bars scattered along the route between the office and the station. Just seeing the words written there – morning set, tuna natto, veal Provençal, green onion salad with vinegar and miso – made me feel for some reason as if I were opening, all by myself, a door that had been closed in my face. With the passage of two or three years, though, everything faded in the most curious way. The things that had seemed most agreeable became objects of disgust: the swarms of people walking, the packed, suffocating trains, the lists of items on the signboards and blackboards in front of the shops. No, that wasn't it. Those weren't what I came to hate; it was the smartly dressed women who walked before me – women of my generation with clothes clipped from the pages of magazines and jewellery that glittered in the sunlight. They had opened the door and walked into a new world.

Watching them always made me feel as if I were still on this side, peering through the keyhole.

And I looked down on them. Through Mother's eyes: *Just look at how they dress! Showing all that shoulder, they might just as well be streetwalkers. And that jewellery jangling at their wrists and throats makes them look like bar girls. The only ones who know anything about Tokyo these days are the ones who've come from the countryside. The men are all pathetic, content to follow after whoever makes eyes at them. All anyone thinks about is eating well and hooking up. It's the end of the world.*

Adopting Mother's perspective made everything seem ridiculous. And that was a comfortable place to be. Just as Mother was convinced I was her, I suppose it was around then that I began seeing myself as Mother, too. We must share something even deeper than our genes.

'It's already five to one,' I say, walking beside Haraguchi. 'This is far enough. You'd better hurry back.'

'It's not a problem if I'm a little late. I may not look it, but I'm a section manager, you know.'

'No, really, it's all right. I'll call you, okay? Thanks again for lunch.'

'Well, as you like. I'll leave you here, then. But listen, be sure to get out of the house more often, okay?'

'All right, all right, I know. See you later.' I wave and hurry off in the direction of the station. I turn and look back. Haraguchi doesn't. He walks away slowly, his massive back receding into the scurrying sea of others returning to their offices.

★

Bonito fillets, shrimp, fresh onions, mitsuba[3] *greens, eggs, butter (the usual brand).* I wander around the supermarket in the department store basement with the shopping list in one hand. Despite it being a weekday afternoon, the store is

3. Also known as 'Japanese Parsley'.

crowded, full of women who look a lot like me. There are younger versions of me, older versions of me, and women my age tugging at children's hands. Each walks with her shopping basket on her arm. Nothing on the floor separates them from me. Each has her own life, and each is living it.

I climb aboard the red train and place the bag from the department store on my lap just as I did a few days ago. The new lingerie had been exciting but the groceries do nothing for me. I close my eyes and feel the swaying of the train with my backside.

I think back to that moment earlier when I realised I probably won't feel lonely after Mother's gone. I've already imagined it many times. After all, if things take their natural course, Mother will die before me. Whenever I imagine her gone, the same scene always comes to mind: the reflection of my pale flesh in the mirror, wearing lingerie I spent a fortune on. Not throwing myself on her deathbed in tears, not the suddenly empty house, not living alone, but me standing exposed before the mirror, wearing only my underwear, inspecting the position of my breasts, the flatness of a belly that has never borne children, the pale skin so long protected from the sun, and the delicate lacy patterns that frame it. There's never been any room in this image for loneliness. And whenever I've imagined this, I've felt a sense of triumph. Not over my mother, but, in some way, over my own life. It strikes me that this, too, is something Haraguchi would probably never be able to understand.

I get off the train and climb the steps toward the glowing portal. The air is comfortably warm and there isn't a cloud in the sky. The trees along the road are dense with green leaves. I cross at the lights and, just past Fujimi Bridge, happen to look down into the Kanda River. Drawn by the softness of the air, I walk along the river in the opposite direction to home. The water in the narrow river below is brown and cloudy. I look down at it as I walk. After a few minutes, I reach Takasago Bridge. Continuing along the river past the bridge brings the hospital into view. As a child, coming this far always left me paralysed with fear. I found the idea that the river continued on forever to be somehow terrifying. So I always turned back at Kotobuki Bridge.

Walking along aimlessly, I turn back at Kotobuki Bridge today, too, and return along the river. I still have no idea how far it continues on. The plastic bags from the department store rustle as I walk.

I stop, press my body against the fence and look down at the muddy water. I imagine tossing the bonito fillets I just bought into the river – tearing open the plastic packaging and releasing the slippery cuts into the flow. I can see the dull red flesh bobbing along in the earth-coloured water. Imagining it makes me want to actually do it. I want to see the dull red fish, lacking head, tail, or scales, swim along in the muddy river. I stick my hand into the plastic bag. Wrapped in an ice pack, the bonito is stingingly cold. I pull my hand back and start to walk again, without releasing the bonito. Just past Takasago Bridge I happen to notice an old woman on the other side of the river, walking slowly with the support of a cart, and follow her with my eyes. Although I have not touched the fish itself, an unpleasant sliminess lingers on my right hand, which I rub on my black slacks as I walk. The fresh green leaves of spring rustle softly overhead.

Mummy

Banana Yoshimoto

Translated by Takami Nieda

A GIRL ON THE BRINK of her twenties will often carry on as though she's figured out the entire world in her tiny little head; I was certainly no exception. She's usually frustrated or irritated for no reason at all. Probably a question of hormones. But sometimes a hormonal imbalance can give birth to an abnormally keen sensitivity. A fleeting brilliance, like a rainbow that arches clear across the sky for just a brief instant. And a select few have the ability to sniff out the scent of others with it.

I was attending pharmacy school and, though I was only two months into the course, I had already grown tired of university. I was feeling glum one evening, cutting across the park on my way home from class, when I spotted a fading rainbow glimmering high in the sky. Then I was struck with a sinking feeling that I may not be able to look up at the sky in this again, not for a while at least.

My premonition proved true. That day, I bumped into a guy at the park – a guy who I'd seen around the neighbourhood – and was abducted, held captive, for a while at least.

I only knew that this guy named Tajima was a graduate student and that he spent half the year in Egypt, working part-time excavating ruins. The well-tanned, mild-mannered man with glasses fit the image of a tutor who might be popular with the girls. I always thought he had nice eyes, so I made a point of saying 'hi' to him whenever I saw him.

'Hello,' I called out innocently and bowed my head slightly.

Tajima smiled and explained that he was out for a walk, taking a break from writing his thesis. 'Someone was murdered here last month,' he said. 'It's too dangerous for you to be walking around here alone. Shall I walk you home?'

What guarantee is there that you're *not dangerous?* I thought, but kept it to myself. 'Is the murderer still at large?'

'Yes, the police even came to our university for questioning,' said Tajima. 'A bunch of us are usually in the lab late at night – with equipment that can be used to chop people up.'

'Was she chopped up? The victim?'

'Apparently. Only the head's gone missing.'

'The head...'

I should have known what was going to happen next – most of the facts were there to see. The truth is, at that moment, as I put my hand to my neck, I read in his eyes what would become of my fate a few hours from then.

But having weighed my options between this acquaintance and some unseen murderer in the deepening gloom of the park, I shuddered at the thought of a killer lurking in the shadows and made what I thought was a rational decision. I chose Tajima and began walking alongside him.

Humans do not have a mating season. We're capable of getting horny in an instant all year round, which is one reason why I decided to go with him. Perhaps I sensed something in the glint of his eyes. Had I been a wild animal, I would instead have been long gone, would have sniffed out the threat to my life. But I was an unperceptive human female, and being horny was all right by me. That moment had been my only chance of escape.

But it was too late. By then Tajima and I were already in the dark shadow of the trees, descending toward our own even darker world.

As we approached my house, Tajima suddenly said, 'It doesn't seem right to just part ways like this.' His eyes were serious.

'Are you suggesting we make a date or something?' I asked. 'Is that what you're getting at?'

He wasn't my type at all. We didn't have a thing to talk about or any common interests. But that feeling of being enveloped by something as I walked next to him… that was it: the only thing that drew me to him. I couldn't picture the two of us meeting at some café near the train station; the idea seemed so ridiculous that I started to walk away.

'Wait, there's something I want to show you.' Saying this, Tajima took me in his arms in the deserted evening alley. He had the withered smell of an old sweater. *If I don't go with him, he'll eventually stalk me and kill me. Either way, this could drag on forever. Let's get this over with.* This was what I was thinking. Or, maybe I just wanted to go with him. Right then, I really wanted some part of my body touching his. I felt his ardour. It was a kind of unpleasant heat I'd never felt before, but something about it touched my soul.

His place was as big as a warehouse, being an actual storeroom that had been converted into a rental space inside the landlord's house. The room had a high ceiling and a ladder leading up to a loft. I sat there all alone as Tajima made us some coffee. I watched the window steam from the boiling water. The room was filled with eerie ornaments. Objects that might have been dug up from an ancient Egyptian tomb. Vases, something resembling an arrowhead, a stone sculpture of a crocodile's head, shards of earthenware.

'What did you want to show me?' I asked, thinking how ridiculous the question was since all either of us was thinking about was doing it.

'Later.' He pushed me down on the tatami mat, as if he'd read my mind.

I didn't like his physique – or the face he made in the act, or the persistent style of lovemaking he'd probably studied from vids – not one bit. He preferred watching me more than penetration or anything else, and didn't seem to think much about pleasing me. But he was so persistent that I came several times, although what I felt wasn't so much the pleasure of normal sex, but a twisted kind of gratification. I don't know how to describe it. The more I hated how strangely slender his arms were, the way the knobs of his spine bulged, how incredibly hairy he was, how long his eye lashes were when he removed his glasses, and how clear his tan line was, the better. The fact that he was silent from start to finish was also a turn on.

The feeling was similar to when I used to go to the beach as a child and lay down at the water's edge. The way the water-softened sand lapped beneath my body. That sensation was pleasant and dreamy enough, but soon the sand gets into your swimsuit, which you know is going to be a pain later, but nevertheless you don't give a damn, so you lie there at the water's edge. You're disgusted until you take the first dip, and then once that soft sand gets a hold of you, you want to linger there forever. That feeling.

After we finished the first time, I climbed naked up the ladder to the loft. He forbade me from contacting my parents and did whatever he pleased with me all night long.

As young as I was, I had my own criterion about relationships: could I fantasize him doing every lewd thing to me or not? If I couldn't, then he was never going to be anything more than a friend, no matter how well we got along. Until now, I'd only dated men who fit that bill. But I'd never imagined a relationship like this – one that existed for the sole purpose of having sex. *You learn something new everyday*, I thought. We didn't talk or take a break. We screwed like rabbits.

Finally, I had to ask: 'When was the last time you had sex?' The question came out of my growing dread of his stamina.

'Only once in high school,' he answered.

Now I get it, I thought.

I wondered what time it was, but Tajima had hidden the clocks, and a heavy black curtain hung across the window. But once I went to sleep and woke up again, nothing seemed to matter anymore, and all I could do was drink water. There was no privacy in the toilet either. I even wet myself once because Tajima had tied me up. Sex is truly a funny thing – the things you don't dare do before your parents and siblings, you can do in front of a stranger you hardly even know. As time passed, I had the illusion that we had always been living this way.

'I wasn't lying about wanting to show you something,' he said suddenly, after I insisted for about the twelfth time on calling my parents before they called the police. He pulled out a rectangular box from behind the neatly organised materials on the shelf. He removed the lid, revealing a shriveled mummy of a cat inside.

'Wow,' I said. 'Did you do this yourself?'

Tajima nodded. I was taken aback. I had meant it half as a joke.

'I really adored this cat. She lived until she was eighteen. So I embalmed her, extracting the internal organs and stuffing her with fragrant herbs, like an Egyptian mummy. I won't bore you with the process, but it took some patience and courage. I was curious to see whether I could even make a mummy myself, but you can't do something this scary on curiosity alone.'

'It must have been a painful process.'

'It really was. You're probably thinking that I did this for fun, but it was very sad and sorrowful and painful. I don't even want to remember. I didn't kill her, but now I'm saddled with a memory that carries the same burden as if I had.'

'I understand.'

'But I really wanted to preserve her. Her form, that is.'

'I'm sure others would want to do the same if they knew how. What you were feeling isn't all that different from people wanting to stuff their pets or knit sweaters with pet hairs,' I said.

After a pause, Tajima said, 'I understand if you don't want to see me again, but will you at least stay another day? You're welcome to call home, if you want.'

'That's impossible,' I answered.

The mummified cat lay there wrapped in a clean cloth. Now that I had glimpsed Tajima's kindness, his character, I couldn't go back to being the animal I was earlier. That impurity called affection had crept into my mind.

My parents used to scold me all the time; I've always had a nasty cold-hearted streak. Once we went to the department store, and the sales clerk knew nothing about serving customers and was so bad about suggesting items to us that my mother decided to go look somewhere else. 'That sales clerk is worse than a cockroach,' I said upon leaving the store, and my parents reprimanded me for thinking such a thing. They cautioned me against looking down on others. But I wasn't looking down on others; after all, I had nothing to be arrogant about. I was only being honest about how I saw the sales clerk. Like a cockroach skittering aimlessly inside a box. This time was no different. I was only being honest. I didn't want to develop any tender feelings for someone I had no intention of dating, so I tried to leave.

'I'm calling home.' I took out my cell phone from my bag, but Tajima snatched the phone away from me and stomped on it with his feet. 'What do you think you're doing?' I got up and headed for the door, but he shoved me, pushed me down and tried to have his way with me yet again. Crushed under the weight of his body, I grabbed a long slender sculpture and brought it down over his head. The clay sculpture cracked with a dull thud. Blood streamed down his face.

At that moment, every concept of love dormant inside me came to a boil. Every feeling of sorrow and longing and incommunicable passion for the people I've loved before and those I will love in my lifetime filled me whole. 'I'm sorry!

What have I done!' I held him in my arms, tears streaming from my eyes.

'It's all right. I'm the one to blame,' he said.

After I cleaned his wound, I called home, told my parents that I'd be away for a few days, and hung up.

Then I slipped into the futon in Tajima's loft, a step closer to love this time.

We made love, careful not to touch his wound.

But the end was nearing. We both knew it.

When I woke up in the middle of the night, I found him sitting up, lit by a sliver of light streaming in from a streetlamp outside. He was staring down at my exposed stomach – hard, as if he were looking at my insides. *He wants to turn me into a mummy*, I thought, strangely unafraid. I fell back to sleep.

The next time I woke up, I heard the pounding of rain. I told him that I would leave when the rain let up, and he nodded. The blood around the wound on his face had hardened. We passed the remaining moments listening to the loud rumble of thunder.

Just how long my parents scolded me, I don't care to remember. My story would have an interesting ending if Tajima had turned out to be the killer, but alas, the culprit was apprehended soon after. It was some deranged middle-aged man who had murdered his mistress before cutting her into pieces.

Tajima and I never crossed paths again. The rumour was that he contracted malaria overseas, suffered a nervous breakdown after returning home, and had been hospitalised, or been going to the hospital on an outpatient basis, or some story like that. I graduated from university, became a pharmacist, and moved out of my hometown.

Several years later, Tajima published a mystery novel set in Egypt and became rather famous, popping up in magazines from time to time. A predictable outcome if ever there was one. He didn't turn out all that great, given how he'd settled for such an obvious profession just because he was smart, liked archeology, and was unusually sensitive. Such an arrogant appraisal of the man might get me scolded by my parents again.

It seemed Tajima had got married, as pictures of his wife appeared alongside him in the magazines. When I recognised, even through her clothes, how similar the woman's physique was to mine, I felt a faint prick in my heart.

I'm in a typical relationship; my boyfriend and I go out on dates, talk about this and that, dress up and go somewhere fancy, make love. I'll likely never lust after someone I meet in a dark alley again. It was a moment when the sensibilities of a younger time became abnormally heightened and turned fantasy into reality. Things are usually comprised of many different angles. But if you remove everything else and take a look at only one world, anything becomes possible. The two of us came together by chance, he responded to my strange inner world with the same energy, triggering something like a chemical reaction, and we both dove into a different realm from reality. Some bewildering intense power must have been at work.

Sometimes I wonder: is this current life, consisting of so many different things, necessarily the correct and happiest one?

The beautiful sound of thunder we'd heard lying on the futon, in each other's embrace, with our eyes open. Perhaps I haven't ever been able to escape the world of that night.

I imagine, for instance, my other-dimensional self turned into a mummy like that cat. I imagine, for instance, the Tajima who died, destroyed by my suffocating love, his head cracked open.

I couldn't bring myself to think that world was so terrible.

The Owl's Estate

Toshiyuki Horie

Translated by Jonathan Lloyd-Davies

I WONDER IF THE two-storey building is still there, inside that dusky residential district, where the rows of wooden houses stretch out from the Seibu line between Shiina-machi and Ikebukuro.

It was a long time ago that I first stepped inside one of the many houses huddled there, past the bend in the tracks near Ikebukuro station, where the yellow trains trundle along at a pace slower than an amusement park ride; back then I had even less sense of purpose or understanding of what I wanted from life than I do now, and I spent most of my time acquiring books, like a second-hand dealer who didn't specialise in any particular variety. I worked for a daily wage and, once I had set enough aside, would use the money to buy books which, eventually, I would on sell for extra money to buy even more books with. As part of this process, one of the tasks I had assigned myself, a *must do,* even if it meant having to stretch a little, was to secure a stock of new French literature, the kind that had no practical use at all.

Tokyo had any number of quality bookshops, yet, while I knew it would be easier, saving both time and effort, to place my orders through one of their well-informed assistants, their prices were sadly too high to be able to use regularly, and would only result in such miserable situations as my orders being detained, maybe for a whole year, while I saved the funds to pay for them.

So I had to get used to the more clunky method of writing direct to wholesale dealers in France, getting quotes for the books I wanted, and remitting the appropriate amount by international money order. Orders from abroad were exempt from the indirect taxation that was usually levied on books so, even inclusive of postal fees, the total cost was less than half that of ordering them from a Tokyo bookshop.

I would pore over the conversion charts for weight and postal charges, adding books I didn't need to the order so as to fill the parcels completely, and this always resulted in orders that consisted of over a dozen books – fairly significant for an individual.

I remember, as if it were yesterday, the shock of discovering that the staff at my local, third-tier post office had not even heard of the system, let alone knew whether they could process such an order or not; foreign remittances were only accepted by the few larger offices that functioned as district hubs. I would drag myself to these buildings, always located next to the larger train stations, and send payment using the exchange rate for that day; then I would wait for the packages to arrive three months later via Siberia. That three-month window could alter drastically depending on the circumstances; sometimes the packages arrived within a month, and one time my parcel failed to turn up at all. I had anticipated this kind of problem when I placed the orders, so I stayed calm and sent a letter asking for redelivery; the dealer was very open about it and helped fix the issue (even though I had not made the order using registered mail), making sure the mess was sorted without any legal ramifications.

In those days, post offices were even more bureaucratic than they are now, and were too stubborn to schedule items for redelivery. Since the parcels were coming by sea, there was no way to know when one might turn up, making it impossible to judge a good time to be waiting at home; this meant I was out for one in every three deliveries, and, each time this happened, the delivery man would wedge a folded notice of delivery into the side of my door.

When I unfolded these, the inscription would tell me they were keeping an international parcel at such-and-such branch of the post office, and that I had to collect it by such-and-such a date. In most cases this meant making the trip to the Toyoshima branch, which was located towards the back of the Sunshine Building. Maybe because it dealt with international mail and people with slips for missed deliveries (or perhaps because the passport agency was inside the Sunshine Building), the relevant part of the building, which was a fair distance from the station, was always bustling with people from many different countries. Each time I visited, I would collect a cardboard package that was as big as I could manage to hold, and then have to trudge back towards the station with it, looking like a beer vendor at a baseball game. Only sometimes, when the books were all different sizes and it was difficult to keep balance, would I reluctantly dispose of this fascinating box, covered as it was with unusual tape and strange customs stickers, with that smell and touch that was completely unlike Japanese parcels, and dispense the contents into a tough plastic bag.

Although it wasn't particularly expensive I was, needless to say, still loathe to spend money on a train ticket in order to pick up something that I had purchased with the express purpose of *saving* money; so, excepting days when it was raining, I would make the journey back to my apartment on foot, struggling with these packages that were completely unsuitable for carrying long distances as I slowly retraced the route of the Seibu line.

About ten minute's walk from the commercial district that surrounded the station was an area of old houses that seemed preserved in time, where two-storey ramshackle apartments of wood and mortar sat close together, and it was here that, fascinated, I would slow from my normal pace to wander through the district.

One time after I had walked the full length of the shopping area – it was lined with taverns, narrow-fronted hardware stores, and unassuming real-estate agents whose buildings resembled the tin-hut lookouts posted near train crossings – already having crossed beneath the elevated rail tracks a number of times, I found myself at the edge of a diminutive square. I continued to stumble forwards, wearing a silly look as I hoisted the cardboard box, together with a large plastic bag I had stuffed with the overflowing books, when suddenly a foreign woman, who I had never seen before, called out to me.

Even to my untrained ear, it was immediately clear that she was speaking in French. I turned to face the direction of the voice, and was amazed to see a young woman standing there, dressed a little suspiciously with what I thought had to be an imitation diamond piercing, about the size of a rice grain, sparkling next to her left nostril; she had compact features and wide-open eyes, with the creased eyelids of a Westerner.

I had never thought I might have to interact with a French national – maybe in Azabu or Hiroo, or near Ochanomizu or Iidabashi with their profusion of language schools, but not here in this outreach of town – and as a result I fell into a kind of daze, momentarily losing all sense of my whereabouts. I was still in this state of shock when the woman jogged up to me and said, 'Hello,' – again in French – then gestured at the large yellow bag that was slung over my shoulder and asked, 'Do you speak French?'

That was when I finally worked out what was happening. Printed there on the bag was the logo of a well-known French publisher of classical literature – a large picture of an owl.

Whenever I made a big order the package that arrived would usually contain a few leaflets, a catalogue with information on newly published books, and a heavy-duty plastic bag that bore the publisher's logo; this proved useful whenever I was out scouring for second-hand books so I often had one with me, folded in four and stuffed in the back pocket of my jeans. I have to admit that the girl's logic was spot-on; any old student in Paris would be aware of the logo, but in Tokyo anyone carrying it around would belong to a smaller, more particular demographic. She laughed, later, when she confessed that she had only felt safe calling out to me like that because she had trusted the air of intelligence the bag had afforded me, and not because of anything intrinsic in the way I looked. I had given a noncommittal answer, assuming she only wanted to ask directions or something similar, so it had caught me completely off guard when she asked if I would, for a moment, accompany her to a take-away sushi vendor that was just a little further on.

I walked with her, uncertain and a little cautious, until the pavement widened into an area that faced the tiny square, with its weak showing of slender trees, that was host to a number of small businesses that included one selling taiyaki,[4] a locksmith and, as the girl had said there would be, a newly opened take-away sushi chain, with glossy fluorescent lights that were stark white and rippling brightly as though under water. I had never bought sushi from a place like this before, so I joined her as she stared wide-eyed at the mysterious line-up of products that had been arranged in neat rows beneath a glass display case – cheese maki,[5] salad maki – but my thoughts drifted away from the sushi to focus instead on her height. In her sandals, she was about as tall as I was. Small, you could say.

'Which are the ones made from soy, the healthy ones?'

I was unable to respond immediately. Even understanding the meaning of the words, I couldn't trace their connection to sushi. It was only when I noticed that one of the pieces on display was labelled 'natto maki', that it dawned on me that this 'healthy and made from soy' thing was natto.[6] It turned out she had been asked by a friend to come out and pick some up from the store, but had forgotten the pronunciation

4. Fish-shaped pancakes, stuffed with bean jam.

5. 'Maki' is a basic sushi roll, usually the wrapping is nori (seaweed).

6. Fermented soy beans.

while reading the map and finding her way. After checking a few times, my assumption seemed correct, so I had the attendant wrap up ten pieces of the natto maki and a further ten of inarizushi,[7] as per her order, then, once she had finished paying, got ready to continue on my way. When we said goodbye and started to move on, we found we were both heading in the same direction, and, after talking for a while longer, it became clear that we lived less than five minutes from each other on foot.

That was when she invited me to lunch, displaying an openness that was hard to believe, telling me they had more food besides the sushi and that there would be enough for me too. When she smiled she had deep, vertical dimples, probably due to the way she drew her slender lips out to each side.

'I'm sharing with an Italian girl. Actually, I kind of just ended up crashing there. She sent me to get the sushi. I'd feel guilty, you know, if I didn't run a few errands for her. Have lunch with us, if you like. Call it an apology for surprising you earlier.'

'I shouldn't. Err… I don't really have much experience with this kind of thing. Thanks all the same.'

'Oh come on, who needs experience to share a bit of lunch? My flatmate's an air stewardess, she speaks French too,' she added, apparently to calm my nerves.

An apartment: inhabited by an Italian stewardess and a young French woman, the kind of girl that was happy to venture into this ramshackle part of town to find sushi for lunch. She had said it was located in the residential district behind the Yamanote Road, and I already had a vague image of the place in my mind. The building would be old and stocky, thick with concrete, thrown up in the last twenty or thirty years; the pillars would have ornamental, onion-shaped caps like those of a mosque, and the balconies would have swollen-out railings that bulged towards the street like vegetation. The walls, needless to say, would be grand and

7. A pouch of fried tofu typically filled with sushi alone.

white. The sitting room would be spacious and full of natural light, fitted perhaps with a beige leather sofa that was firm so it wouldn't sag under the weight of the long-limbed Italian stewardess as she sat down, and there would be a low, clear-glass table arranged before it. Would I sit there, I wondered, timidly grazing on the sushi once it had been laid out on the spotless table?

'I came to Japan from Australia. It's been two months now, but I only moved into this apartment the other day. So I don't know my way around the area yet.'

'Ah, I had assumed you were French.'

'No, I am. I'm just studying abroad, at a university in Australia. I'm here for the holidays; tourist visa, of course.'

When, in this way, we had come to chat more easily with each other, the girl – perhaps out of guilt as I stumbled along, grappling with the large box, as sweat collected on my forehead – offered to help carry the plastic bag with the picture of an owl, the one that had enabled our chance and unexpected meeting. I was still jumping at shadows, fearing some hidden agenda as we continued on our way, but after 15 minutes or so, when we turned into one of the remaining side-streets, the girl pointed at one of the buildings and exclaimed, 'This one!' My fears dissipated the moment I saw it. I had expected a dense, heavy building, something completely alien to the usual mass-produced apartment blocks with their thin walls, something not necessarily pearly white but close enough to it, yet what stood before me was a thoroughly battered wooden apartment on two storeys, with an American-style communal post box balanced on a thin iron pole, before a north-facing entranceway with space enough to park a number of bicycles.

The patio door opened to reveal a shoe cupboard to the left and, on a stand above the wooden step leading into the house, a pink phone; a shallow, dimly-lit corridor stretched into the building from the sunken entrance area for taking off your shoes.

'I had pictured something a little more… glitzy. You did say you lived with an air stewardess.'

'Ha-ha. Actually, we prefer this kind of thing.'

On hearing the door, a largish blonde woman poked her head out from the kitchen to the left of the corridor and, judging from her sweatshirt – red and white with a tin of Campbell's Soup on it – and the way she had it casually tied around her waist, I guessed she wasn't the Italian. The French girl chatted with her in English for a while, then she introduced me, telling the girl I was a sushi chef.

'Come to mention it, I still haven't asked your name,' I said, as though the thought had just occurred to me; the French girl laughed and apologised, telling me her name was Isabelle. The girl in the sweatshirt looked like she was having a hard time gauging our relationship but, at the same time, had apparently taken Isabelle's claim that I was a sushi chef at face value, and seemed to want to interrogate me further on the subject; but we couldn't even shake hands, as hers were already full with a kitchen knife and a potato. It transpired that the Italian air stewardess had been called out while Isabelle was shopping, and had left a message saying she wouldn't be back for a while, and for Isabelle to go ahead and eat without her.

It seemed that, in my unexpected appearance, I had ended up taking her place. Showing me into her room first, Isabelle said, 'Well, the two of us should be able finish this off at least,' then she followed the girl in the sweatshirt back to the kitchen to make some tea.

Isabelle's room – actually, the room she shared with the Italian girl – was around six tatami mats in size and located towards the end of the ground-floor corridor; pale light streamed through a single window across from the door, looking out to a modest back garden. Contrasting with my impression from the corridor, the room received a good amount of natural light. I seated myself on the yellow, sun-faded tatami, and took in my surroundings; the only furniture to speak of was a small folding table, on top of which was a

Walkman that had been attached to a pair of miniature speakers to form a makeshift stereo system, and three or so books in Italian, all stamped with library markings. A pale-green sheet was draped over a couple of mattresses towards one corner of the room, allowing them to double-up as a sofa during the day. There was a tapestry on one of the walls – picked up in India, Isabelle told me later – with an image of Buddha in the weaving, and suspended from the window frame, a wirework basket full of tools for burning incense. There was a half-broken reading light that looked like it had been scavenged from a nearby tip for bulky household items, suspended from a plastic cord which was itself draped, artlessly, over a hook screwed into the lintel; there were no lights in the ceiling.

I had not been inside a proper Japanese room like this for a long time. My apartment at the time was Western, the kind with an actual bed, and even beforehand I had always put down carpet to cover up the threadbare tatami of my other dirt-cheap apartments. I realised I was close to forgetting the way exposed tatami felt underfoot.

I sipped at the black tea Isabelle had offered me (completely overturning my expectations, I had been certain she would make green tea) and restrained myself from commenting that it didn't really complement the sushi, then I helped myself to some of the latter all the same and listened to the agreeably low timbre of her voice as she explained the mysterious building's set-up.

The basics of what she told me were that people learned about the place via word of mouth, that it provided budget lodgings for foreigners staying in Japan on short-term tourist visas, and that people preferred to call it the 'Ijinkan', or 'Foreigner's Estate'. It lacked all the annoying red tape that came with renting a normal place – guarantors were unnecessary and rent was calculated on a daily basis so tenants could come and go whenever they pleased. The building itself was antiquated at best, with a communal kitchen and only the nearby public baths as bathing facilities, but the low cost, combined with the flexibility it offered for coming and going, meant that it was highly regarded all the same.

It was apparently due to the landlord's altruism that the place was as welcoming as it was to foreigners, and apart from Isabelle, the current tenants included the girl in the sweatshirt that I had already seen, another two Americans, the Italian girl Isabelle shared with, a Chinese girl, and a Mexican. The only Asian, the Chinese girl, turned out to be a devout Catholic that everyone jokingly called *Madmoiselle Chretienne*; she was, Isabelle said, curiously antisocial for someone that declared a love of humanity, but people mostly kept their distance and apart from her everyone else got along fairly well. Until a week ago, there had also been a German girl sharing with the Americans on the first floor.

Except for the German and the Chinese girl, who were both students at local universities, everyone was here as a tourist, Isabelle included.

'Even so, you did pretty well to find a place like this.'

'We have a special information network. A really complex network that doesn't reach Japanese people. When I first got here I was supposed to be sharing with the American girl in the kitchen. But I took one step into her room and... Oh my god! You'd never think the room was a girl's. I'm fine with most things, but not *grime.* I had half given up when, as luck would have it, Francesca's partner – that's my roommate – decided to go back to Italy and a space opened up in here. Maybe it's only the lack of things, but it feels pretty roomy in here, right? I had a hunch Francesca and I would get along, so I made the pitch and we ended up sharing together.'

Isabelle had studied modern literature at university in Lyon, then taken a job with a market research company where she worked for two and a half years. The work involved meeting clients and there were lots of business trips so it was perfect for someone like her, who liked interacting with other people, but one day she had decided enough was enough and broke into her savings to go travelling.

She went to India first, then Colorado in America (using the contacts of an American she had met during her time in Bombay), and from there she flew to Australia. She had planned to stay until her tourist visa expired, but after a friend's urging had ended up enrolling at university in Sydney. She had not originally taken English with the explicit aim of studying abroad.

Still registered at the university, she was visiting Japan for her summer holidays, although she said she didn't know how long she might end up staying for. However it went, she would need to make a trip abroad and come back again, and soon, as her visa was close to expiring. Deep down I thought it all sounded a little hackneyed, the kind of thing people in Japan did during the 60's or 70's, but I warmed to her anyway, mostly because of how she related it all without any apparent awareness of how typical it sounded.

'I was amazed to see people bowing their heads like that, when they greeted each other,' she said.

She had already known about Japan's so-called 'culture of bowing', but instead of thinking the practice odd when she saw it first-hand, she had actually been impressed and even jealous about the way people showed each other respect – what an amazing country, she had thought – but after this she had been shocked again when she witnessed the chaos of people getting on and off the trains. 'I couldn't believe it… Why would everyone get so crazy like that? I knew they were all like you, decent men and women that would help me out if I stopped them in the street to ask directions or something, but I don't know… they just *transformed.* And then, the moment these people who have been in a total frenzy actually get on board, what do they do but start to *read,* in silence. It's madness. Let me tell you, French people don't read that much. Those people were all smart, so I can't understand why they would behave so disgustingly, and only when they were on the platform.'

Her insights into Japan were limited to general observations, and I was starting to feel like I was studying the correct way of having a stereotypical conversation with a visiting foreigner, but she *had* recognised the owl logo so I took a leap of faith and brought up the subject of Roland Barthes and his writings on Japan; when she responded, however, it was unsurprisingly with a stock answer: 'I've heard of him, but I haven't read his work... I'm more a fan of his voice than I am his books. I have a tape recording, an interview for a radio programme – no matter how much I listen to it, I'm always captivated by that gloomy, elegant voice. I'd love to read the book, though, especially if it's got something to do with bowing.'

'I'll bring it by next time, as thanks for the sushi,' I said.

I was still struggling to wrap my head around the fact that I was in the room of a foreigner – a girl I had only met an hour earlier, with whom, having finished a meal of natto maki and inarizushi, I was now doing my best to converse sensibly, and in a foreign language I had only a scant understanding of. I reflected on how, if I had not chosen this day to pick up my surface-mailed parcel, if I had taken the train instead of trudging back on foot, if my timing had been off by even a minute, I would probably never have met this youthful and somehow peculiar girl. If I had been carrying just the box, and not the bag as well, she would not have known what was inside: even if she had still called out to me, I doubted she would have used French.

When we had eaten our way through most of the sushi, a smallish American girl came down from the first floor, on her way out with a rucksack on her back, and popped into our – *Isabelle's* – room for a quick hello. She was a healthy-looking girl of average height and weight, and introduced herself as Jessie; she seemed genuinely interested when I told her I was a sushi chef, showing off silver-wired dental braces with an open smile.

I decided this might be a good time to take my leave and had got partway to my feet when Isabelle's roommate turned up, coming in just as Jessie was leaving. She looked incredibly tall. Her figure was impressive but she was horse-faced, making it hard to imagine her as an air stewardess. I got to my feet and made to shake her hand: Francesca – the name seemed worlds apart from her stern-looking features.

She made quick work of the three pieces of natto maki Isabelle had put aside, and had just finished gulping down the remaining cold tea from Isabelle's cup when she said, 'Emergency call, from mama-san[8] – I'm needed at the club tonight. I did have plans – such a pain to cancel, but what can you do, huh?' Her thick-boned shoulders came up in a shrug.

'Oh, really? You had extra last week too, I bet someone's asking for you by name.'

'Yeah, mama-san said one of tonight's clients has a thing for tall girls.'

I couldn't help noticing that the conversation had moved in an odd direction. 'Sorry, what's that about a club and a mama-san?' I tried.

'It's a tough life, honey.'

'Yes well, whatever it is, it sounds dodgy to me…'

Isabelle shot Francesca a look and, after obtaining the latter's silent permission, calmly outlined the situation. She explained that most of the lodgers in the building had part-time jobs at an upmarket night-club in the Akasaka district.

'Don't get me wrong, we're not prostitutes. There's a members-only club in Akasaka, with all kinds of CEOs and executives as clients. Anyway, these guys seem happy just to have foreign girls sitting next to them. We work part-time, a couple of days a week, on different nights. I'm also teaching at an English school, but the club is *hands down* the best way to cover the cost of living here. Really though, all we have to do is sit next to these guys and nod on cue. There's nothing underhand going on, it's a cinch.'

8. The title 'mama' means female owner, landlady or proprietress.

'So that thing you mentioned, that "special information network", I suppose you meant the mama-san at this club? Let me guess, she's the landlord?'

'Exactly. This is her place.'

Isabelle was the only French girl at the club and, if her own words were to be believed, her friendly nature and petite size had gained her quite a following. She had written to her mother, explaining she was earning close to 400,000 yen a month from a part-time job that needed only two days a week, and her mother had responded with a fierce admonishment, misunderstanding her as having started work as a prostitute.

I was hardly surprised to hear that a parent would become worried upon learning that their daughter, who they had assumed was concentrating on her studies in a great nation of the Southern Hemisphere, had actually washed up at some island country in the Far East and was now working there for a living.

I had, by this point, worked out the reason why the building's tenants were all female, but I couldn't help also noticing that almost all of the people Isabelle had mentioned, the people the landlord had so *graciously* gathered here, happened to be Western. They might have all been working here on tourist visas, but the situation for *these* girls was entirely different to those from South-East Asia, who gave up on their own lives for the sake of their families. The system that supported Isabelle and the others was a pimp-like remnant of the boom-days, of the bubble economy when Western women who were looking for a good time had flocked to Tokyo, becoming products for consumption, paragons of health that bore no relation to ideas of suffering or self-sacrifice and who were replaced in short, three-month cycles. This was also why, regardless of what she might have actually wanted, the Chinese girl on the first floor was marked from the outset as being external to it. The reason given for the regular switching of the line-up, namely that it was a safety measure to prevent clients from getting too attached to the girls, was, I suspected, just a pretext for another motive, one which had nothing to do with protecting the establishments and their reputations, and everything to do with concealing the existence of these girls who earned a living on tourist visas.

Once the story had formed in my mind, it was as though a noxious odour had swept into the room.

On my way out I hauled the cardboard box into my arms and stood there, as ridiculous-looking as I had been on the way over, while Isabelle used a blue rollerball pen to write the Ijinkan's phone number on the lid. I wanted to return the gesture but my hands were full so I recited mine verbally; she copied it onto the pad next to the pink phone, then circled ahead to slide the door open. I thanked her for the unexpected treat of sushi and said I would come back with the book soon.

Two days later, I used the excuse of an evening walk to carry the Barthes paperback across to the Ijinkan. Jessie answered when I called from the entrance, dressed in a way I couldn't say was demure; she told me Isabelle was at her fitness club in Shibuya, and that she was supposed to teach English at a school in Azabu at night so they weren't expecting her back until late. I gave her the reason for my visit and asked her to pass on the book for me, then continued with my walk.

Upmarket nightclubs, fitness sessions, language schools.

I wondered what Japan would look like to Isabelle and the other girls. It might have been relatively easy for Westerners to find work in Tokyo, but it didn't feel like something to be proud of, not if the city was just a conduit for enjoying the high life, even if it was only on a short-term basis.

Putting aside my lack of knowledge of how other countries worked (I knew very little), I still felt uncomfortable about the way this influx of foreigners was being marketed as evidence of an increased cosmopolitanism, even though they were only passing through, and only via backdoors that were like cheats in a computer game. But my thought processes lacked the viscosity of natto maki and the vinegar lucidity of sushi rice. My understanding was limited to generic flavours, and I didn't have the necessary creativity to give birth to new, previously unknown classifications of sushi. That was perhaps why I was unsuccessful in garnering more information from interacting with these people in the flesh, and talking in a foreign tongue, than I could from reading something in print.

I was in bed one morning, three-or-so days later, lazing around and continuing a book I had started the night before, when Isabelle called me to ask if I could accompany her to Azabu. Her contract was for private English lessons, but a potential student had requested lessons in French and was scheduled to meet her later on that day to discuss the lesson format and terms of payment. Isabelle explained that this person was a complete novice and understood no English, and then, just like that, she asked if I could help her out by tagging along as a kind of interpreter. I certainly wanted to believe her story, especially when she went so far as to say she would put a word in with her manager to get some work put my way if I agreed. Luckily, I had the day off from my part-time job so, for the second time, I said yes, keeping my sights on the benefits a little interpreting work might have on my financial situation, and ended up accompanying her to the school, located in what was, for me, a completely alien part of the city.

We got off the Hibiya-line train at Roppongi and made our way down a hill beside the wall that surrounds the Defence Agency, before crossing an empty park to an area that was flush with high-end apartments.

It goes without saying that it wasn't the owner of the Ijinkan that had introduced Isabelle to her job as a language teacher; it was, instead, the man that had met her at the airport, who had helped her find accommodation on the day she arrived in Tokyo (essentially, I gathered, a complete stranger – some distant acquaintance, like a friend of a friend of a friend). Looking back I can see that there was at the time an incredible momentum behind the proliferation of language schools, and an almost unlimited demand for private lessons, regardless of whether the teacher was qualified. Isabelle had started off giving private English lessons to a variety of businessmen, but after her manager had belatedly realised she was French, he had skillfully reeled in a number of new students for her.

'The school's such a weird place. They market themselves as having this system where they find teachers to meet whatever needs their students have, covering all the languages, but it's just the manager, this really cunning guy, setting up parties each month: he invites a bunch of locals and foreigners based in Tokyo and says the parties are for 'promoting international exchange' when, actually, they're to sweet-talk people into working as teachers. That's how I got started. And Francesca too.'

I had assembled a pretty good image of the place by the time she had finished and, sure enough, the 'school' she taught at turned out not only to lack its own building, but also its own classrooms. It rented space from a hotel that let out the majority of its lower-occupancy rooms on apartment-like leases, and scheduled its classes in shifts, on a day-to-day basis; when one room wasn't enough they would convert another they used as an office into a makeshift classroom, and would sometimes even use the coffee area in the hotel's lobby.

Aside from the management, the organisation only retained a couple of female receptionists who worked on rotation, thereby maintaining a scale that allowed it to disband easily and at short notice, and nothing I saw suggested that significant flows of capital were taking place behind the scenes.

Isabelle was due to meet her new student in the lobby at 3.30 that afternoon, and then inform her manager once the lesson content and other terms had been confirmed. We arrived a little behind schedule and waited for the young woman, who was apparently travelling from Yokohama. When she was still to arrive by four, however, Isabelle began to fret about what might have happened, insisting she hadn't made a mistake with the time or venue of the meeting. The school office was closed until six, when the phone receptionist came in and, besides, there was no reason to suspect the woman might have gone there instead. The woman had her details, and should have been able to get in touch via the hotel's front desk. When there was still no word by five, we were forced to conclude that she had either forgotten about the appointment, or that something important and unexpected had come up instead, and decided in the end to call it a day.

Isabelle had started complaining to herself about how the woman should have picked a day when she had other lessons, and so, hoping to distract her, I brought up the subject of the book I had dropped off with Jessie the other day. She gave me a dimply smile and said she had read about half, then outlined some of her opinions on the work, including how she thought it would be interesting to compare the portrait of the man in the book with Barthes' later work on photography, and, while it was certainly *possible* that the portrait was just another example of the many 'signs' he had seen scattered throughout Japan, she considered it altogether more likely that Barthes had chosen the man simply because he had fancied him.

'You know, an old friend of mine used to have a Chinese boyfriend who looked exactly like the man in the portrait. They broke up when my friend left him for a Frenchman, of course. There's something strangely erotic about that photo, don't you think?'

'I suppose there is, now you mention it.'

'I'm pretty sure Barthes didn't chose him at random, you know, not with cheekbones like those – he's being pretty obvious about it, really.'

When the conversation dwindled, Isabelle told me she was going to head to the gym to work up a sweat and clear her mind, so we waved each other a quick goodbye at the ticket gates inside the underground station.

After that, I was busy with work and had no time to get back in touch, although I had assumed she would call before too long because she still had my book. As with the woman from Yokohama, however, I heard nothing for two, then three weeks. I began to worry that she might have got into some kind of trouble, and she had mentioned her visa was about to expire so, on a Sunday afternoon, I decided once more to visit the Ijinkan, again using the pretext of a walk. The corridor was noisy and, when I called out from the entrance, the American girl with the Campbell's sweatshirt poked her head out from the other end.

When she caught sight of me she said, 'Ara ara',[9] using some Japanese she must have recently picked up, before switching to her usual, laid-back English: 'Isabelle and Francesca both moved out, last month.'

'Isabelle… moved out?'

'Yup. We've got a couple of new tenants in the end room.'

Stunned, I tried to ask where she had moved to, but the girl insisted Isabelle hadn't told her anything. I pushed my way upstairs (I didn't really need to go that far, I suppose, but there was still the matter of the book) and knocked on the door that said *Jessie,* her name written with magic marker on a sheet of coloured paper.

I was surprised to find that she had been drinking, despite the fact that it was still the middle of the day. She was flushed and her white skin was covered with blotchy red spots, and when I stuttered through my questions all she did was laugh and say things like, 'Aiii donn know.' I did my best to stay serious and ask again but she only said, 'Shee… sheleft,' slurring as she spoke. Gesturing with my hands and body, I tried to convey to her that I found it hard to believe Isabelle would get up and go without saying anything, especially considering they were all such good friends. 'I think… she left her jobbat the club… and the language school… so maybe she's gone back to Australierr,' she said, maintaining the same expression, and actually making some

9. 'Well, well!'

sense, before dissolving into a fit of giggles.

'Not that Francesca and Isabelle left together,' the Campbell's girl – who had followed me upstairs – added calmly, picking up where Jessie had left off. 'Francesca was first; she went back to her old job.'

'Her job as an air stewardess?'

'Ofcooorse… shedid!' Jessie hollered.

I followed the Campbell's girl downstairs, and she let me use the pink phone at the door to call directory services for the number of the Nogizaka hotel; when I got through to the front desk they forwarded my call to an organisation that rented a room and had a name that suggested it might be a language school, but no one picked up.

I guessed that if Isabelle really had left, they would have already found her replacement. What I needed was her forwarding address, but if she had left the job without giving them any details, then I had no means of finding it out.

Had she been lying when she said she got on well with the others? Or were the girls all hiding something by sticking to this story, only pretending that there was no message or, indeed, book? A couple of Americans had, it seemed, already moved into the six-tatami room at the end of the corridor, so I couldn't really go barging in to see if she had left it there.

For whatever reason, Jessie had trailed downstairs after us and at that point I must have looked utterly dejected because she took me by the arm and said, 'Fancy some tea?' inviting me up just as she stumbled over herself, forcing me to prop her up; I glimpsed something yellowish – cheese or cereal, or bread – stuck between the wire of her silver braces. I remembered how, years earlier, many of the kids I had known had been forced to wear horrific braces.

Does it hurt to have solid metal pressed against your teeth like that? Is there a special way of brushing your teeth? Don't your teeth and gums rot from all the food caught in the wires?

Such were the stupid questions that used to pop up and block my thoughts whenever my brace-wearing friends opened their mouths to smile, sometimes dulling my reactions so badly I couldn't even respond to things they said. I hadn't paid too much attention to Jessie's mouth the last time so the fact that my eyes were being drawn there now was no doubt a sign that I was getting a little worked up. Her breath carried a strange smell, a mix of sake and Listerine that came together in a vile but minty stink; it was a smell I had never imagined before, and had no words for.

I followed her – *helped her* – back to her room, which was so full of smoke I could only make out a white smog. I sat her in a corner, trying to avoid toppling us over, then took a proper look at the others in the room. I saw a couple of redheads – not the girls from the day I had first met Isabelle – each the image of the other and partying noisily, drinking beer and sake and other things. They alternated between crossing their legs and throwing them to the side as they sat, and both had square, strong-looking shoulders; judging by the volume of cans crushed in front of them, they had already consumed a substantial amount of drink.

Natto maki and inarizushi one day, then sake the next, I thought, incredulous, as I immersed myself in this unattractive scene, while an alien language darted this way and that. I decided that I would wait, and pretended to sip at the glass of whisky Jessie had insisted on; occasionally I looked for an opportunity to get up and excuse myself, but one of the redheads – who was lying on her side, wearing cropped trousers that showed off legs covered in fine hairs, like the kind on a goat's stomach – kept peering up at me, firing out a rapid succession of sentences, the whole time creasing up with laughter (I knew she was speaking in English, but I couldn't understand a word) and this gradually broke down any confidence I had in being able to get back up: eventually I heard her say something that sounded like 'milk' and gave her an ambiguous nod in response, inadvertently prompting the red head on my right to grab a carton of soy milk from a corner of the room and start decanting it into my drink.

A useless memory came into my mind as I rushed to stop this act of goodwill, something from years ago, a spate of TV adverts that had audaciously suggested adding milk or raw eggs to the energy drink *Oronamin C.* Once mixed with a cocktail stick, the drinks had been exactly the same colour as the soy-milk whisky in my glass: I took a sip, not knowing what else to do.

I wondered if these lively girls, who were partying in a narrow six-tatami room with the windows all but closed in the middle of the day, also attended clients at the landlord's nightclub.

The redhead to my right was wearing a white T-shirt with a yellow banana motif, and each time she jogged her torso up and down a couple of dark points would move in time, jiggling underneath the fabric as obviously as a finger poking through, making it impossible for me to know where to look; it was no better the other way, as Jessie was doing the same to my left.

'So what're you… hic… doing here anyways? Azabu's the place to go if you wanna study English. You g… hic… got someone you're sweet on here?' the redhead to my right asked, belching as she did and, in response, Jessie said, 'He's a sushi chef. He lent a book to Isabelle and says she never gave it back,' also hiccuping.

'A book, to a girl? What a nerd!' the redhead exclaimed, clapping her hands again and barrelling with laughter. I tensed in case she tried to grab me, but she quickly reverted back to her earlier crazy gossip. I didn't know what it was that she found so funny, but whenever anyone strung even a few words together she would fold up in hysterics, pressing her thick legs (I was sure they had twice the bulk of mine) up against me.

I kept a nervous eye on the pair of redheads, who kept saying 'You know!' to each other, as if to confirm my initial impression they were identical in every way, just like twins, from the colour and style of their hair to the clothes they were wearing. They had the same rounded nostrils that were long and thin, elongated mouths that opened wide enough for a fist, and broad slender eyes.

I wondered if they were *actually* twins.

I sat with my legs crossed in a vague attempt to look

masculine, desperately concentrating on staying afloat among the rush of words, when the redhead to my right (who for some reason had been regularly topping up my milk, even though she carried on like I wasn't there) piped up and yelled, 'Hey, watch this!' giving her hair a sudden tug and transforming it in that instant to a shade of hazelnut, surprising me so that I accidentally tipped my glass over the tatami. I wanted to say *Ah! It was a wig*, but I couldn't remember the English word. As ignorant of wigs as I am, I was surprised to see that the hair underneath seemed greater in volume than the wig itself, and then even more surprised to discover that the strands of hair, shining in the sunlight that poked through the smog, were all split and forked into two branches. Those with a single split were actually the better ones, for each time her head swung in close and I was able to steal a glance, I was given an unimpeded glimpse of hair that was bunched and matted, with vine-like strands that had split multiple times, seeming overly-fertile as the branches angled off in all directions.

'Is your hair fake, too?' I asked the other redhead, who was sitting in front of me and so wired I couldn't help wondering if she was smoking something stronger than tobacco. She giggled and pulled at her hair before leaning in, almost crawling over the bottles as she came closer, gesturing for me to try it for myself. Guessing it unwise to take a handful and yank out a clump of her hair, I pinched a few strands between my index finger and thumb and gave a slight tug: the reddish hair popped out with an audible snap, all the way to the transparent root.

'Ouch! You actually did it... You went and pulled out my hair!' she laughed angrily, 'Now you have to give me some of yours too.' She came closer still, now on all fours. Again the English for *I didn't mean to!* failed to emerge, leaving me helpless to defend myself amidst a sudden chorus of purring cheers.

Where the hell was Isabelle? Why wasn't she here when I needed her? Why was the Campbell's girl still downstairs?

Just then the sliding door burst open and another

blonde girl came crashing into the room with a large paper bag in her hands, shouting *Kinkado Banzai! Kinkado Saiko!*[10]

By the time it dawned on me that she was shouting in Japanese, she had plunged her hand into a garish plastic bag and, as though scattering confetti, had begun to launch handfuls of bunched-up fabric into the pallid smog. As the strips rained down from above, price tags dancing in the flurry, Jessie, the redhead and the girl with the hazelnut hair all launched themselves forwards, shameless as they attempted to grab them before they hit the floor, in the process kicking over the cans of beer and the soy-milk whisky next to my knee, spilling them all across the sun-faded mats. For a moment the liquid seemed like it might be absorbed, but, instead, it skimmed along the surface, carried by the residual gloss of the rush matting as the objects came to rest, small triangular shapes, now a pile in the centre of a broad stain.

'Sylvia, how many did you buy? You're crazy buying this many… when would we ever need all of these!' Jessie cried as she wheeled around, but the girl she had called Sylvia only yelled some more – *Kinkado Banzai! Kinkado Saiko!* – hurling even greater numbers of the delicate fabric products into the air. They were black, beige and pink, with bargain-bin stickers plastered over price tags that were still attached like good-luck charms, occasionally opening up to reveal their true shape, like nocturnal birds in the cacophony. I just sat there, sticking out and surrounded by their endless laughter, unsure when one of the 'redheads' barged into me whether I should do something, and I forgot completely about Isabelle and the book as, instead, I gazed vacantly at the fabric shapes that had become attached to the tatami, watching them darken as they sucked up the murky liquid.

---

10. 'Kinkado forever! Kinkado you rock!' Kinkado is a store selling clothing and fabric goods.

Dad, I Love You

Nao-Cola Yamazaki

Translated by Morgan Giles

IT IS A MYSTERY to me that sympathy is an emotion common to all people. When you're down, those around you will always urge you on. A near-stranger you would never tell your worries to suddenly showers you with kindness. Like sunlight pouring down on you.

Someone ran up to me on the platform when I was on my way to work.

'You dropped this.'

She handed me my wallet. A black synthetic leather wallet. So full of receipts that it bulged.

'Thank you very much.'

Blindsided, I bowed and when I took the wallet, the woman, somewhere in her sixties I'd guess, grinned.

She was on her way to work – food service, probably. Her hair, speckled with white, was pulled back in a bun and she wore a tracksuit top; beneath it a navy blue apron peeked out. You might commute in your apron if you worked somewhere in a station, like the kind of noodle place where you eat standing up. The woman went back to the end of the queue to board.

I must have dropped my wallet when I'd pulled it out. I'd abandoned it and it had been returned.

I put it away in the inner pocket of my briefcase.

Picking up a thing someone had dropped. It was as if it were an everyday act, but it was something precious. I was stunned. As if I might cry. Mentholatum smeared onto the wounds in my heart.

Why is it that people pick up other people's things? To make a connection? To give a little kindness to someone who feels down? As a way of saying, *I accept other people*? The world is held together with such generosity.

My wife had run off a month before. It seemed likely that we would separate, but for the last thirty days, I'd done nothing, just gone to the office as usual. I hadn't heard from her since.

I worked in the operations department at a research agency. My role was Acting Section Manager. We would receive requests to compile figures and reports on popular opinion and the work backgrounds of directors, and then sell-on the information. We primarily dealt with companies related to textiles. Thread wholesalers, cloth manufacturing companies, clothing retail stores and the like. The heart of our research is listening to conversations. That was my job.

Getting off the train, I headed toward my office block.

As I was walking down the street, I suddenly stopped dead. Thinking nothing.

What is life for? I started working here 22 years ago; I'm 44 years old. Fifteen years left until retirement. For the last month I'd been living with my daughter, just us two. My daughter is called Yukari. She's eighteen, in her first year at university.

The elevator took me to the seventh floor, which smelled, as always, of shampoo. Why is that, I wondered? What is that smell? Is it the way the women in my company smell, or the detergent in the kitchenette, or the smell of formaldehyde?

Saying 'Good morning,' to the people I passed, I headed for my department's section. I'd arrived at my desk.

After running my eyes over the newspaper, I made tea and started making research reports. When I was interrupted in the middle of compiling them, my consciousness fled in the opposite direction from work.

If my heart was able to be free, I was fine, no matter what cubicle I was put into.

When I thought about my wife, an uneasy feeling came over me, like I was disappearing from my knees downward. My thoughts were such that I felt like I really couldn't live, like my chest hurt. It was as if the calcium in my body had dissolved and I'd become a mollusc. A feeling like a well gone dry.

But even if, say, my wife wished I were dead, I was here and I had to go on living.

When people all over the world, throughout history, have already had these same problems, why do we have to deal with them all over again? We could all live a lot longer otherwise. It would be more efficient if, from the start, there were a set number of people that existed and we could all grow up together. This system where the old die, new children are born, and we start again from 'A' seems so stupid.

With this sort of thought in my head, it was already twelve by the time I finished three reports. I heard the bell.

At my office, at the morning and afternoon break times and at the end of the day, a bell rings. It's the 'Westminster Quarters', *ding dong ding dong*.

At that, a female employee called Ushiku who sits a few desks over came up to me.

'Would you like to eat lunch with me?' she said. Ushiku had joined the company two years ago, so she was around 24 years old. She had a baby-face and black hair, and with her plain style of dress, she seemed at first sight to be slightly younger.

'Sure.'

Although I nodded without giving it deep consideration, I thought, *What a strange person.*

Ushiku grabbed her grey pocketbook which had some lettering that read 'Miu Miu', put on her coat and, briskly and without hesitation, walked to the elevators. I put my own wallet in my pocket and followed. We left the building and waited at the lights at the scramble crossing.

The manga artist Fujio Akatsuka had died; the comedian Tamori was still doing the show, 'It's Okay to Laugh'. Change and no change.

The clouds were ruffled like a mackerel's scales; above them, the sky was pure blue.

We crossed at the lights.

I saw ahead two stylish boys walking hand in hand toward us. They were about 21, 22. Students probably. One was built like a model and wore casual clothing. The other was rugged. A serious-seeming youth, he wore a plain white t-shirt with jeans. Were they lovers? This was the first time I had seen two men holding hands like this, I thought.

The sunlight was dazzling. Taking it in, I felt my heart being uplifted.

For lack of anything else to do, maybe I'd start going to the local park every morning, to read a bit before going to work. The morning sun would hit me as my eyes passed over line after line of writing. If, after ninety days of doing that, I didn't feel like I could go on living, I could kill myself. But I would probably want to go on living.

Letting Ushiku lead, we walked down a big road for a bit before turning right onto a small street. There was a Thai place, like a food stand.

There were two waitresses. They wore dark blue t-shirts with an elephant print and an apron tied around their waists. Both seemed Thai. In broken Japanese, one said, 'Welcome. Party of two?'

'Yes,' I said, and we were led to seats.

At the table next to us, the man was seated on the bench against the wall, and the woman was sitting in the chair on the aisle. Seeing that put me at ease. There are so many rules now that didn't exist in the old days.

Lately, pseudo-chivalrous rules had taken hold in Japan; now wherever you went, women were seated by the wall and men were on the aisle, all in a row. This felt forced to me. There was this pervasive, unspoken pressure that if you went somewhere with a woman, you had to let her sit in 'the seat of honour'. Although it doesn't feel very different at all, wherever you sit, there was now this feeling that it was 'bad' for men to sit by the wall. Although conceding the bench seats to women was only a formal constraint, we couldn't even use our facial expressions to convey, 'I have concerns about this.'

While my thoughts drifted, Ushiku said, 'Please,' and pointed at the bench, sitting in the chair herself. So I sat on the bench.

'I've never really eaten Thai food before,' I said.

'How are you with spicy food?' Ushiku asked.

'I love it.'

'And cilantro?'

'What's that? Someone's name?'

'No... Um, how about *tom yum kung*?'

'Someone else's name?'

'It's the name of a dish. It's a soup.'

'Let's get that.'

'Shall we do a tapas kind of thing?'

'Hm... What does that mean?'

'Get a few things and share them.'

'Let's do that.'

Ushiku called over the waitress from before and ordered tom yum kung, *khao man gai*, and *som tam*.

'I find it difficult always being surrounded by women. I thought, why can't I just go to lunch with a man without it being a big thing?'

Certainly I couldn't understand the reason for the custom of only going to lunch with co-workers of the same sex either.

'Why indeed.'

'Women ask each other to lunch like it's nothing. We have our packed lunches together. But it's really clique-y.'

'Huh. That's terrible,' I said.

Tom yam kung is a red soup, not as spicy as it looks, but sour instead.

'At three, you have to put out some snack,' she said. 'There's some sort of order, and when your turn comes up you have to buy a snack and bring it in. This is among the girls in the group. So on the day when you say, 'Oh, is it my turn?' you get something not too classy, but not too boring, decently tasty, and that comes in individual packs so it's easy to share, and then you have to divvy it out to everyone. It's that kind of situation.'

'Aha. You don't share with anyone else?'

'I don't know why, but there are group politics.'

Khao man gai is chicken with rice. The rice is sticky. Recently the Japanese government had banned the import of foreign rice, so it wasn't Thai rice but *koshihikari*.

'Ms Ushiku, you're pretty good friends with Mr Yamada, right?' Since I had killed the conversation, I asked her a question. I had occasionally witnessed Ushiku and Yamada talking, seemingly happily.

Yamada had been in the sales department since joining the company eight years ago. He was about thirty, and for whatever reason he was disliked by his female co-workers. Maybe it was his hairstyle or the way he acted, or maybe it was because he gave off the sense of being what society calls the 'Akihabara-type', a geek. Also, when he was talking to someone, Yamada couldn't look them in the eye, making him a bit suspect, and sometimes he stuttered while speaking. Maybe people thought of him as someone who's not good in social situations.

'Yamada's a really great guy,' Ushiku said.

'I think so too. His work is very carefully done, with very few mistakes.'

'And he really pays attention when he talks to you.'

'Yes. He gives it his all.'

'I'm going to get behind people who give things their all, I've decided.'

'Oh?'

Som tam is green papaya salad. It has dried shrimp and peanuts on top. It is tremendously spicy.

'Even people I don't get along with in the slightest, if they work hard, I'll give them my support. So no matter what kind of people I'm around, if someone's giving it their all, I'll support them.'

'I see.'

'So, say we're playing football. Even if the game is boring, even if it feels like the teamwork's just not there, if the ball comes to you, you kick it full force – that kind of thing. That's the kind of person I want to cheer for. I want to back people who give it their all.'

'So even if that person is a really clumsy person, even if they break up the harmony?'

'I'm behind them.'

'You really mean it.'

When we'd finished eating and paid the bill, the waitress said, '*Kob-khunka*,' to us in Thai. I didn't understand what it meant, but I replied, 'Kob-khunka.' The waitress laughed and, watching us leave, said, '*Mai pen rai*.'

It was still only 12.30 when we left the restaurant.

'Shall we get some tea before we go back?' Ushiku asked.

'Sounds good,' I said.

'Is it all right if we go somewhere a bit trendy?'

'Sure.'

And then, because we were going to a trendy café, I was nervous.

I pushed the yellow wooden door and entered. Everything had a hand-made feel, or a European feel, but anyway, it gave off an atmosphere of wood and cloth.

It was a dim place, only lit by the sunlight through the windows.

Eighty per cent of the customers were women. And, in the main, they were young. Only at the table next to us were seated two elderly people, a man and a woman. They were both most likely in their eighties. The man wore a tie around his thin neck. The woman wore a black suit over her plump body. Both were in funeral clothes.

The woman was seated next to the wall and the man was on the aisle. So I sat in the chair this time as well. Ushiku sat on the bench seat.

I ordered coffee and Ushiku ordered something called 'chai'.

When I looked around the café, I noticed that each chair was different. Was that fashionable? The floorboards looked like they had been intentionally left unwaxed. On the ceiling, there were luxurious fans rotating, like you see in European movies.

On top of the table, there was a little vase not much bigger than my thumb with no more than 30ccs of water in it, and in it, some leaf that I couldn't help thinking they must have found by a roadside.

'What does that taste like?' I asked, looking at the thing Ushiku was drinking.

'Sort of like… sand,' she told me.

'Have you eaten sand before?'

'Not really, I guess.'

'It's gritty, then?'

She chuckled. 'The texture is smooth. It's not that, it's the flavour. It's… like dust, or it makes me feel like I'm in the desert.'

'Huh.'

'Haven't you ever wanted to describe something as tasting like something you've never tasted before?'

'I have. "This water tastes like cement," or something like that. Although I've never licked cement.'

'Right. How does that kind of comparison even come to mind?'

The coffee was good.

Not long after, when Ushiku stood up to go to the bathroom, I started listening to the conversation of the two old people at the next table.

'It really does seem like we met in another life.'

These two in their funeral clothes stood out in the fashionable café, but their voices blended with the quietly playing bossa nova. They were discussing their pasts and their futures.

'Wakaba, do you have any brothers?'

'I have three older brothers, but the one closest to me, Ken, really doted on me. I was very small and he looked out for me. When I was growing up my father always told me, 'Wakaba, when you were born, you were so small, you could fit in my hands. From head to toe, you fit in the palms of my hands.' I was less than a third of a kilo, three hundred grams – I was born premature. But despite that, I grew, which I'm glad for. When I think what my parents must have felt seeing such a small baby, I'm glad that I grew up normally.'

It wasn't clear to me how they knew each other, but I gathered that they had lost a mutual friend and encountered each other at the funeral for the first time in decades. The woman and the man each seemed to have a spouse, but neither had come, so it seemed likely the deceased was not a relative. Both used formal language, and both seemed not to know anything about each other's lives, so they could not really have been friends.

The phrase 'the doctor' kept coming up in their conversation. 'So-and-So from my department at university,' 'at Dr So-and-So's hospital….' Maybe they knew each other through a hospital. There were points when I would've said she was a friend's sister from when he was in medical school, for example.

'I never would have imagined we'd meet again like this.'

'Me too. I seldom come into Tokyo.'

'Do you have any children?'

'I have two sons. They've already left home. It's just me and my husband now.'

'It's just me and my wife now too, all on our own. My daughter is in Hokkaido.'

'Somehow, it feels like we're meeting after our own death.'

'It really does, you know. I feel like we're lazily talking in a field of flowers. I'm glad I got to see you today.'

'Mm. Because we never know when we'll see each other again.'

'We'll see each other in heaven, without a doubt.'

'Do you think you'll recognise me?'

'Of course I will. I'll call out your name right away. "Wakaba, how about a cup of tea?," just like earlier. You know, Wakaba, your face hasn't changed a bit over the years.'

'No. I'm all doddery.'

'No, you haven't changed.'

'Oh, I'm embarrassed now.'

'If I invite you for tea again in that world, will you join me?'

'Yes. I think I'm likely to go before you, so I'll be waiting.'

'Certainly not, I'm going before you do. I'll get us a table. How about a fashionable café like this one?'

'People as old as us feel a little nervous in places like this. In the land of the dead, let's go somewhere slightly simpler.'

It was then that Ushiku returned.

'Sorry for keeping you. Shall we head off?'

I looked at my watch. It was 12.55.

'Oh, lunch is over.'

'We'd better hurry.'

'No, we can take it easy.'

I paid the bill.

When we got outside, I felt like I had just been born. Like, *What is 'being able to see'?*

My eyes were blurred by the dimness of the café. The mid-afternoon sun was invigorating.

When we crossed the scramble crossing, I saw someone

who looked like my daughter Yukari. I quickly lost her in the sea of people, but that image of Yukari floated in my mind.

Soon I became concerned about whether Yukari was all right or not. Maybe she'd been in an accident, or become ill and collapsed.

I prayed to myself jokingly: *Please – the sun, temples, some obscure god.*

I took the elevator to the seventh floor, split off from Ushiku and went to the toilet. After I'd finished, I sent Yukari a text message that said: 'Are you OK?' A reply came quickly. 'What are you on about?' Relieved, I put my phone in my pocket, went back to my desk, and started the afternoon's work.

At four, I went out to visit a Chinese-run company out in Ogawa. It was within walking distance, so I printed out a map from the internet and looked at that as I went.

The office was in one room in an apartment building.

'Come in.'

The president was a tremendously beautiful Chinese woman. She was probably in her forties. Being alone in a room with a pretty woman caused me no end of anxiety.

The company was an e-retailer selling women's clothing, and the room was bleak, with nothing but a solitary computer and rack after rack of clothes on hangers.

'We have received a request for information on your company, so I would appreciate it if you could answer my questions to the best of your ability.'

'A request? From whom, I wonder.'

'Basically, it's against policy for me to tell you who requested it.'

'Oh my.'

I started the questions. Gradually I asked how long she'd been selling here, about what she'd been doing before founding the company, about her customers.

She gave me perfect answers, padding the sales figures and inserting lies about the company's history here and there.

'Thank you very much,' I said to express gratitude, and she sighed audibly.

'The truth is, it's not going very well. Business is tough. Especially for a foreigner like me,' she let spill.

'It must be hard to do it all on your own.'

Taking the lead from her complaint, I comforted her and shared information about the business world, as much as I could tell her.

The last thing she said was, 'It's really difficult to gain someone else's trust.'

'It is,' I said. 'You can only build it little by little. And only through honest efforts.'

Then I said thanks again, and headed back down the road I came on.

My office building shone.

Its walls were illuminated by the setting sun, and all the people working within it were being blessed.

After I had performed my routine tasks for a while, I started wanting a cigarette. There was nowhere to smoke inside the building, so smokers went outside. Outside the entrance there was an ashtray. By the roadside, there was a line of vending machines selling cigarettes and canned drinks. The sky was suddenly the colour of night.

I took the Mild Sevens out of my pocket and lit one. I wasn't a heavy smoker; I went through half a pack a day.

Not long after, a woman in her thirties and a man in his fifties came, smoking Marlboro Light Menthols and Cabins, respectively. They weren't from my company, but they definitely worked in the same building. The woman wore a beige suit and the man was in grey. They had ID cards from different companies hanging around their necks.

We smoked together, the three of us.

After putting the butt in the ashtray, next I wanted to drink a canned coffee, so I took out a hundred yen coin from my wallet. Just then my hand slipped and the coin fell onto the pavement. It rolled on its edge, going under the vending machine.

'Oh,' said the man in his fifties loudly.

'It's just a hundred yen,' I laughed, embarrassed. 'Never mind.'

'No. Don't give up so easily,' the woman said, crouching on the road without even taking care to hike up her skirt. She brought her cheek close to the ground, straining her eyes in the dark space.

'Is it there?' The man asked, getting close as well.

'I can see it. Something round and silver. But it's very far back,' she said, squinting.

'Well, you can't get it then,' I said. 'Let's give up.'

'No, it's fine. I can get it. Do you have a stick?'

The woman would not quit.

'How about something like this?'

The man picked up a wire-like, thin stick and handed it to her.

She took it and stuck it in the gap, moving it around.

'This bends too easily, I can't get at it. Is there anything stiffer around?' she asked.

'But, really, it's just one hundred yen. It's all right.'

I gave up arguing.

'How about this? No good?'

The man picked up something like a broken bit of a blind, like a metal spatula.

She took it, smoothly sweeping it across the ground.

'Oh, almost got it, almost got it,' she whispered.

'C'mon!' the man cheered her on.

'Whoa, there it is,' she said, as the hundred yen coin came shooting out from under the machine.

'Yes!'

For some reason, the man pumped his fist in the air.

The woman stood, adjusting her skirt. 'Here you go,' she said, handing the hundred yen coin to me.

'Thank you very much. Really.'

I bowed to the two of them and, still gripping the coin, I went back in the building. It was embarrassing, but I didn't really feel like a canned coffee anymore.

You need other people, to give your own life a sense of purpose. No, that's not it. People just want to be close.

I left work after seven.

When I got home, my daughter Yukari was at the dining room table, resting her chin in her hands.

The end of her ponytail, done up around her cowlick, was in her fingers. The hood of her parka was inside out, the back of her neck swelling outward.

'I'm home, Yukari,' I called out.

'Welcome back, Ikuo,' she said, glancing toward me and raising the corners of her mouth for just one second. She always called me Ikuo.

'I'm going to go change.'

As I went to pass by, Yukari stood right up. 'I'll warm up the rice.'

'Mm-hm.'

I went into the room I used as my own, a Japanese-style room, and took off my necktie, changing into sweats.

I hadn't changed the tatami mats in a long time, so the rushes were beige. The parts of the paper-panelled door that had been broken were plastered with sticky tape.

When I went back into the dining room, Yukari was just dishing up the miso soup. Her denim-clad legs swished around as she worked. The way she moved hadn't changed a bit since she was a child.

'I'll get the rice, then.'

In a daruma-patterned[11] rice bowl and a rabbit-patterned rice bowl, I heaped white rice, as densely and as appetizingly as I could. There were two lights on the kitchen ceiling, but both were dead and had been left that way,

---

11. Also 'dharma'; a traditional, hollow, round doll modeled after Bodhidharma, the founder of the Zen sect of Bhuddhism.

because I couldn't be bothered, for a year. In the dim light, Yukari brought the plate of miso-pickled mackerel, the small plate of pickled radish, and a little bowl of seasoned boiled spinach to the table and said, 'Let's eat,' handing me chopsticks.

I took them and said thank you.

'I don't know how good this is.'

'You don't have a club meeting tonight?' I asked.

'It's only Wednesdays and Saturdays,' Yukari said, putting a fish bone on the edge of the plate.

'No classes?'

'I had three today.'

'Oh.'

All the side dishes were bland. I'm originally from the Kansai region so I like bold flavours, but all the meals that my Kyushu-born wife made were basically bland. Yukari's cooking was even blander than her mother's.

'What was that weird text you sent me this afternoon about?'

'I passed by someone who had a face like yours on the road near my office. That's all.'

'So, but, what does that mean, "Are you all right?"'

'I wondered if you were all right. I was worried.'

'Of course I'm all right. You saw me this morning.'

'Maybe you'd been in an accident and were in trouble.'

'How would I have been in an accident?'

'It's not too much work for you, making dinner?' I took a sip of the enoki[12] miso soup.

'Not at all,' Yukari said.

'Oh, I saw that Kyu has pulled out.'

Kyu was the nickname of a marathon runner who had announced his retirement. The news had become a topic of conversation.

'I was so shocked.' Yukari looked down.

'Why?'

12. Also 'enokitake' or 'enokidake'; a long thin mushroom.

'It's just a big shock that he's pulled out.'

'But he's already given his best.'

'But quitting like that, it sucks.'

'When someone who's given it their all until the end retires, they'll be in high demand. As a commentator, as a coach, everyone will want him. He'll get lots of invitations to give speeches, too.'

'Hmm.'

Looking as if she did not comprehend, Yukari crunched on a bit of pickle.

'Knowing when the time is right is important, you know.'

'Oh?'

'It takes a certain amount of style to quit when the quitting's good.'

'I guess so.'

I should mention that although Yukari is mine and my wife's daughter, we are not connected by blood. I first met Yukari when she was five years old.

After we finished eating, we washed the dishes together, and I took my turn in the bath first.

I got out of the bath and was lying down, reading the newspaper, when I heard a voice call from the garden, 'Ikuo!'

'What?' I yelled.

'Look. The moon is huge,' Yukari yelled back.

'All right.' I was annoyed.

'What's wrong with you? You should see this,' Yukari said loudly.

'I'm tired,' I replied, closing my eyes.

'C'mon. You really gotta see this,' Yukari said, continuing to draw me out.

She wouldn't stop, so forcing myself up, I opened the sliding door and put on my slippers.

Yukari had a short jacket on over her parka and was standing in the center of the garden, pointing at the sky.

'Look. The moon.'

The moon was big and white, exactly as if it were from the Heian era. I was definitely surprised. But I muttered a noncommittal, 'OK, I've seen it,' and looked away.

Yukari hit me with the question: 'Why is it that there are some nights when the moon is big and some nights when it's small?' She looked at the moon with all her focus, her breath coming out white, warming up the black night sky.

'You know, I don't know. Maybe the atmosphere acts like a lens. So maybe there are nights when the lens is thick or thin,' I replied, without much thought. Huh. It really was a mystery why the diameter of the moon changed every night.

'Why is it? Why?' Yukari kept asking, like a child.

'I don't know...' I said. I was cold so I slipped out of my slip-ons and went back into the room. As I did, Yukari whispered at my back:

'Dad, I love you.'

For some reason I could not reply, my voice was frozen. It was all I could do to turn my head and grin at her, and I quickly returned to my room.

I stayed hidden in my futon.

In the alcove in my room, there is a hanging scroll.

A picture of a waterfall. A white waterfall, like it's flowing with noodles. It's not intended as realism, but looking at the water, parts of it make you think, 'There are times I've seen water move like this.' The kind of mountains that in fairytales are made by mud dripping from the feet of giants.

Like water falling, it is only after a person's feelings and relationships are in place that the shape of things is clear.

Every night, I can't really sleep.

But it's great – just being alive.

Just by being alive, my rallying cry becomes: 'I am against suicide.'

Every morning, just by opening my eyes, I express this.

'I am living in this world.'

It echoes throughout my body. 'I want to be alive still.' 'I want to experience the world.'

Just by blinking, I accept the world.

When problems at home or relationships at work get strange, every morning you can take in the air through your nose, feel the sunlight rest on your eyelids, feel your bed with your fingers.

Just being alive – it's great.

That I just continue to be alive is great.

Morning is absolutely beautiful.

Mambo

Hitomi Kanehara

Translated by Dan Bradley

I WONDER WHEN IT began. When I started imagining sex with every man I laid eyes on. Imagining kinky play with the geeky men I'd pass by. Or getting covered in sweat as I grappled with every chubby man I'd see. Imagining sex in the missionary position with a towering convenience store clerk, and wondering whether I'd be impressed by the height difference and how much I'd have to look up during the act. Having my teeth drilled at the dentist's and imagining myself strapped into the examination chair and the dentist penetrating me with a speculum. And how, during this daily occurrence, my breasts would swell from a D to an E cup. I'd gone to a lingerie shop, just in case, and that's where I learned the truth.

'That's impossible,' I said, 'I'm a 65 D.'

But the shop assistant said, 'No, you're an E.'

Does that mean your breasts get bigger if you think of nothing but sex? Maybe if you keep on thinking about sex, your body responds by releasing large amounts of hormones, and it's because of these hormones that my breasts have grown bigger. I'm looking for men the moment I step out the door, imagining our affairs, and I usually get wet and my breasts expand. So what on earth is going to happen to me next? What am I evolving into? Perhaps, at this very moment, I'm transforming into the leading figure of some great female revolution. Or maybe everyone else is just hiding it, and women have always found that their breasts grow bigger when they're in heat. I don't understand. I don't understand my own sexual desire.

'Utsui?'

'Yeah.'

'My breasts have gotten bigger.' I'd finally managed to say what I couldn't say before, afraid of being treated like a weirdo or called a liar. Utsui, still gazing intently at the video game screen, responded with a bone-headed 'Huh?' *Is this it?* I thought. My boyfriend of three years already. I began picking lint from the carpet.

'When you say "breasts", d'you mean "breasts"?' Utsui asked me in a throw-away manner, like he was distracted, but I didn't know what he meant. Utsui's good points were his face and his muscular chest, and his bad points were saying the occasional staggeringly narcissistic thing and, as he just had, not listening to what you were saying.

'What does that even mean?'

'Huh? "D'you mean breasts?", you mean?'

'Yeah. What did you mean, "D'you mean breasts?"'

'Hmmm. Yeah, I wonder what kind of breasts I meant.'

'Well, I mean breasts are breasts, aren't they?'

Utsui let out a troubled hum as he struggled on the brink of death. As he delicately hammered on the buttons he would let out an *Ah!* or a *Woah!* If the task was arduous – trying to lift some heavy lever up and down, or turning some gigantic handle like the rudder on a boat – I might see him differently, but the task involved tapping on small control pad buttons, so Utsui looked like a monumentally stupid human being. I wondered if I was the only person who thought a fully grown man screaming as he tapped on tiny buttons was as frivolous as someone trying to buy coffee from a vending machine, but getting cola when they press the button, and then angrily calling up the vending machine company to make a complaint.

'I wonder if those buttons would be too small for Americans.'

'Huh?'

'That control pad, right, I wonder if it'd be too small, like, from an American point of view. The buttons, I mean.

People over there, their hands and fingers are bigger, aren't they?'

My words were brimming with sarcasm – *you are a small, pathetic man*, I was saying – but he had no idea. Not that I was going to measure whether anything was big or small, of course.

'Right. They've probably got controllers just for Americans.'

Buttons. Nipples. And clitoris. I can't stop moulting. My lint. Lint. And clitoris. I think it would feel great if, one day, my eyes popped out and were snatched away like lint. Perhaps my clitoris's physical response to the word 'clitoris' in my head is another part of my evolution. As I lay spread-eagled on the carpet, I stared at the ceiling and recalled the roughly 50 men I had slept with that day and, out of them, I remembered the great sex I'd had with a man around 40 years old who'd been dressed in a suit, sitting by the window of an Italian restaurant on Namiki-Dōri Street. Neatly cut short hair, tanned skin, a suit of gleaming material, a yellow tie, a wristwatch, probably a Bulgari, and a Vuitton key case. Yes, he was slick and middle-aged, but the second round in his Merc parked on Namiki-Dōri Street was great. As I straddled him on the lowered car seat, riding his face as he licked me, I looked out through the back window and saw a young girl wearing a yellow hat, waiting with her father at a traffic light crossing. I watched the two of them holding hands as they crossed the road, then disappear beyond the line of gingko trees. The tentative licking grew ticklish; I couldn't keep my hips still and I moaned gently, so he sped up the movement of his tongue. At that moment, I remembered being at elementary school and the rule that the first year students had to wear a yellow cap when walking to and from school. On the back of the cap was sewn a handwritten name tag that said 'Year 1 Class 2: Yū Kanda', and I would often look at the characters and think how if I stared just hard enough at 'Yū', the first character from my name, it would start to look like the character for 'Wa'. And why was it only first years who had to wear caps? Maybe it was because first years were more likely to be run over by a car. More likely, it was to remind them they were at the bottom of the pecking order, by making them the only ones who had to wear those caps. Because if wearing a yellow cap protected children from car accidents, then everyone would think it was a good idea for all children up to Year 6 to wear them. The birth rate has tragically shrunk in recent years, so maybe they've passed a decision so all children have to wear them too. The number of children wearing caps. The precious role assigned to children who wear yellow caps. As I gasped at the feel of his tongue on my clitoris, this was what ran through my mind. The man then stimulated my clitoris with his right thumb while he flicked his tongue in and out of my vagina. I remembered that for the past few months, for no particular reason, I'd started using the Washlet bidet to wash down there. Maybe it was all about soliciting this kind of encounter. I can't trust my own sexual desire. This desire that has swollen my breasts. As my hips began to tremble, the man, almost spitefully, started to increase the pressure. I raised my legs, climbed off the man and sat myself down, still naked, on the back seat, and then he stimulated my G-spot with two fingers and, in less than a few minutes, I came and ejaculated. I always made sure I was well hydrated so that I could gush whenever I wanted. Using the bidet was an unconscious thing, but staying well hydrated was deliberate. I probably rated my special ability to gush in large volumes a little too highly. But I loved that I could squirt such large amounts. I would intermittently tell the man to stop when, really, I wanted to squirt so much I couldn't bear it. Because whenever I squirted, it made men happy. Maybe this is me passing the buck? Or maybe this was a convenient thought. With sex, it feels like it can only be conducted through these vague unspoken communications; that this is what the other person expects, enjoys or wants. As he saw my cum splashed on his suit trousers he laughed in amazement, arousing my sense of shame, then he pulled his fingers out and made me lick them. As I started to wonder if the back seat was soaked with my cum and if the stains would stay on this leather upholstery… the man had taken off his trousers and penetrated me. His penis felt thick and heavy. It occurred to me that this tightly packed organ was just like a white-skinned sausage. As I put my mouth on his shoulder to stifle my voice, the smell of his sweat and the texture of his skin stimulated my tongue between my lips. I noticed several strands of white hair along his hairline. Whenever I embraced a man like this, face-to-face, I always noticed his various details. The watch I had thought was a Bulgari turned out to be a Zenith. The stubble that looked coarse was actually soft. The smell of fresh bodily fluids wafted around the car's interior.

'So what happened? Why did they get bigger?'

'Huh? Why did what?'

'You said your breasts got bigger.'

'Oh, I dunno. But the lingerie shop assistant said it was probably because I was in heat.'

'You're lying.'

'Of course I'm lying! It's the service industry, no shop assistant would say anything that rude.'

'Yeah, you're right. So what were you saying? Don't animals and things like that get bigger breasts during mating season?'

'Hmm, I don't know. But tons of hormones are released, so it might be possible.'

'Yeah, because with monkeys, their bums turn red, right?'

'Oh, really? Yeah, but talking about bright red monkey bums is not exactly cute, like in that kid's song.'

'Yeah. Humans evolved from monkeys too, right? So when women wear red lipstick it's a sign that they're in heat.'

'Oh, really? So how do you explain the popularity of beige lipstick without any tinge of red over the last couple of years?'

'...That would be a sign that women have stopped wanting to have sex with men.'

I watched Utsui fighting the boss as he said these things, not knowing if he was serious or joking, and I realised I could no longer imagine having sex with him. It'd already been two months since we'd slept together. For the first time, I'd started to understand what people meant when they said they 'had cobwebs down there'. If I don't have sex for more than a week, the inside of my vagina starts to fill with cobwebs. If it was an empty cave, it would probably be smothered in thick fog. And for the first time, I had respect for whoever coined that phrase. The people who used it must feel hollow. Thinking about anything other than sex right now made me feel hollow.

This was the first time I'd felt this way, in the 20-something years I had been alive, and now whenever I tried to think of anything other than sex, I was overcome by the vision of my entire body sprouting dense fresh green moss and becoming part of a Japanese garden. To prevent this, I had become a body incapable of thinking about anything but sex.

As I lay on the carpet in the shape of a cross, staring at the ceiling and listening to the background music from the game Utsui was playing, I remembered. I'd gone to McDonalds to order from their Breakfast menu and was asked once more, 'Was that a Sausage & Egg McMuffin?' and I said, 'Bacon, Sausage & Egg McMuffin,' giving my order to the man for the second time. He was wearing a paper hat and when I embraced him I realised for the first time that it was fixed to his hair with a short hairclip. I'd always thought it odd that I'd seen so many of these little hats riding on people's heads and never once seen one slip or fall off, but now I'd managed to save time solving a problem that had puzzled me for years, without even meaning to. In the McDonalds male toilets, the man stifled his voice as he penetrated me from behind, while reaching in front with his right hand to cover my mouth. The hand was clammy and stank of oil, or whatever they use for fries, but that's what you get with a McDonalds employee. As we were still dressed, I raised my hand from the hem of my skirt and put it on top of his, which was massaging my breasts underneath my jumper, and I squeezed even harder. Perhaps he was the one who had made my breasts bigger. But I'd only thought about this for a moment before he came, after only three minutes, leaving me disappointed.

'I couldn't go again today,' I said.

'Huh?' said Utsui.

'The psychiatrist.'

'Oh, right. I see. Is that OK?'

'It's not OK. I haven't been for ages.'

'Is the reason you can't go, like, psychological?'

'Don't you think it's odd saying something is either psychological or physical? Because I don't think they can be divided or separated that easily. It's like, Utsui, your shoes and shoelaces being classed as separate things. No, maybe that's too hard to understand. What I mean is, look, take mammals, right? Dolphins and whales and people are the same – they are all mammals. It's like you can ignore the size and weight – it makes no difference because we're all the same, you know.'

I don't think I'd been to the psychiatrist for several months. That's several months of thinking I'm gonna go, I'm gonna go to the psychiatrist. And how many times did I dress myself up, how many times did I leave the house and lock the door behind me, how many times did I catch a taxi or ride a train or ride my bike or take a walk so that I could get to the psychiatrist? After going to McDonalds that morning and having sex, I had a hearty meal, then sex with that skillful guy on Namiki-Dōri Street, and then while I was having sex again with several other men I checked the Jorudan train route-finder on my mobile to work out how to get to the psychiatrist, realising I'd have to change lines if I got the train, and so decided OK, I'll get a taxi, and it was while I was waiting at the taxi rank on the main road that I met him. The man looked over 50; both his beard and his hair were peppered with white hairs, and he seemed rather absent-minded. If you had to put it nicely, you'd say he looked interesting. To put it less nicely, he was a hopeless case whose special gift was looking creepy. He was casting shifty glances in my direction but I quickly realised, as he gazed far down the road, that he must have been waiting for a taxi too. He seemed to be in a hurry, fidgeting and occasionally yanking a tightly grasped fist up to his chest in irritation at the complete absence of taxis. I moved a little distance away down the road, as if to say, No big deal, I'm not in much of a hurry, if a taxi comes you can get in it first, even though I've actually been waiting here much longer than you, because the last thing I want is to get into a nasty fight with someone so, honestly, it's fine. But as I did so, he shyly approached me.

'Excuse me, are you waiting for a taxi?'

'Yes.'

'How long have you been waiting… for the taxi?'

'Um… I've smoked three cigarettes so about six, seven minutes.'

'Ah, I see. Oh, I'm in such a hurry.'

'Oh really. If a taxi comes, you can get it.'

'Ah, but, that would be so rude of me.'

I don't know whether it was agitation or nervousness but he spoke in a strange way with this embarrassed expression on his face. I started to enjoy inspecting this flustered-looking man, and held his gaze.

'So, where are you going, Miss?'

'Er… how about you?'

'Seaside Park.'

'Oh! What a coincidence. Me too.'

I wondered if this kind of coincidence was actually plausible, but then again, the lie was unlikely to be exposed, and even if it was, so what? It was probably a poorly thought-out lie, though, to be honest.

'Oh, really?' he said.

'Yes.'

'Well, shall we go together? Split the fare. Because it probably costs a lot to travel there from here, right? Isn't this perfect?'

'Yes, that sounds fine. It is a coincidence, yes.'

'Yes, well, a coincidence indeed! This is only the second time I've gone to the Seaside Park in my entire forty-eight years. And yet, in the middle of going to Seaside Park for only the second time in my life, to meet someone in Shinjuku who is going there too, well, it's the kind of thing that will probably never happen again as long as I live! This experience today makes me feel like you do just before you die and your memory flashes before your eyes.'

'Ah, is that right?,' I said. I spoke in a way that must have revealed my discomfort and repulsion because the man sank into silence like he regretted even opening his mouth.

He stared down the road once more and mumbled, 'Well, it's no good, there's not much traffic around here.'

I began to regret lying about going to Seaside Park. For one thing, it was miles away. And it was clear to me that I was going home full of self-loathing because I'd finally left the house to go to the psychiatrist but had nothing to show for it, and that sharing a taxi to Seaside Park with the first strange man I met, just the two of us, was idiotic.

'Shall we walk a little?' he asked. 'Perhaps we can wait where there are more cars passing by.'

'Yes, you might be right,' I said. 'They probably won't come here any more,' following the man. It occurred to me that, aside from Utsui, it had been a very long time since I'd walked side-by-side with another man and, strangely, considering the kind of guy he was, it wasn't unpleasant. He was repulsive to look at, but, for some reason, he didn't make my skin crawl like elderly or homeless people did. It was probably the combination of thick beard, sideburns and menacing deep black pupils that gave the reassuring impression that he was like a small animal. But I couldn't help feel there was some sort of disturbance dormant in those eyes. I bet this man had an incredibly odd-shaped penis. As I walked with him, I couldn't stop my gaze from darting around the area between his thighs. The area around the crotch of his corduroy trousers suddenly grew long and sharp and I thought I was going to squeal. I'd never seen one like that before! But no sooner had I thought this, I realised it was just his index finger thrust inside his pocket. I suddenly sensed the colour drain from my face and I looked up. The man was giving me a cold stare. 'What is it?'

The instant he asked me that question, the whites of his eyes showing, I realised; our roles had been reversed. This man thought I was a pervert. Obviously, my daily routine *did* involve imagining having sex with every single man I passed on the street. 'Nothing', I said, and looked away. I could see a security guard in uniform walking on the other side of Namiki-Dōri Street. In a flash, the guard was inspecting my belongings, frisking my whole body, stripping me naked, using his finger to search inside my anus and my vagina, and after the back of my throat had been investigated by his penis, I was thrown out of the guard's office with my clothes and belongings, my mouth still full of semen, and the moment my bare back hit the cold floor, my mouth twisted and one long string of the security guard's semen oozed from between my lips.

'It smells bad, doesn't it?'

'Sorry?'

I asked the man again what he meant and he asked me if I could smell something bad.

'What kind of bad smell?'

'Well, it's a feline sort of musk,' he said.

'Isn't it the gingko trees? The pavement round here lately is often covered with fallen gingko nuts…'

I got this far and then I held my tongue. Perhaps this man was provoking me. He suddenly raised his voice and called out 'Taxi!' in a shrill voice and managed to stop one that had its 'For Hire' lamp lit. 'Please', he insisted, 'after you.'

I said nothing about how much I felt I should probably just go home, and I got into the taxi.

The man got in the back and said, 'Seaside Park, please.'

'Huh?' the driver replied in a stupid voice like a bean rattling around a washbasin.

'Which Seaside Park would that be?'

'Seaside Park is Seaside Park, of course!'

'No. No, I think there are several.'

'Oh, really? What about you, Miss? Which Seaside Park are you going to?'

I cocked my head and mumbled something like, 'Oh, I don't really know,' and waved my hand as if to say, what about you, Sir?

'I was just told, Come to Seaside Park at two o'clock, but I don't think they said which Seaside Park.'

'Ah, I see. Because I wasn't directed toward a specific one either. Driver, any one is fine so, for the time being, please just take us to Seaside Park.'

'You can say, "For the time being" all you like... but which Seaside Park do you want to go to?'

'Seaside Park is Seaside Park, of course!'

As the man insistently repeated himself, the confounded taxi driver looked at me and his eyes pleaded for help.

'Sir, who are you going to meet?'

'My ex-wife.'

'Oh, I see. Well, you can't be late for that, can you?'

'That's right.'

'Well, what if you tried to give your ex-wife a call?'

After the taxi driver had offered this reasonable solution, the man said, 'Ah, well, but I don't carry a mobile phone, but perhaps I can borrow one?' He took out his pocket diary and began thumbing through the pages.

'That's fine,' I said, 'but the battery is running out…' I passed the man my phone and he punched in the numbers while he looked in the diary.

'…Ah, hello? What? It's me, Kaizu. I'm just borrowing someone else's mobile phone. Because mine has stopped working. Speaking of which, I'm in a taxi right now, you see, and, well, where is Seaside Park?… Yes. Wait, *not Seaside Park*? Oh, you meant the Sunshine City Aquarium? The one with the Mambo fish? That's right. But why did… Huh. So why on earth did you tell me to go to Seaside Park?… What! You said it yesterday! So what should I do? Because right now I'm sharing a taxi with someone who is going to Seaside Park, too. What should I do now, then?… Because if I say that, it'd be rude, that's why. What? Yes. That's right, but the taxi driver has no idea where it is… What?'

'Look, it's fine, I'll get out here. Please go to Sunshine City Aquarium by yourself, Sir.'

'No, not at all, that's no good at all. It's fine, I will get out instead.'

I had been noticing for a while now that whenever he referred to himself he would swing from using the childish male personal pronoun *Boku,* to the casual *Ore,* and then to the polite gender-neutral *Watashi.* Is this an adult man? And whether Kaizu was a family name or a first name, I had no idea what it meant. Maybe it was written with the same characters as the Aizu region.

'Well, I think I will get the tram after all. There's a tram that goes to Ikebukuro, right? I've found the underground no good lately. Yes, I'll take the tram. I'll probably be running a little late but you will wait for me, won't you? Sorry, you sound far away, is everything OK? Have you been eating properly?… Hello? What?… Hello?'

As the man muttered in confusion, a beeping sound started coming from his hand.

'Oh, the battery has run out,' I said. 'I'm sorry, I forgot to charge it yesterday. Well, shall we do that, then? It looks like I'm not going to make my meeting at Seaside Park, no matter what I do, so please take this gentleman as far as Sunshine City Aquarium and I'll go home by myself afterwards.

Sunshine City is on my way home anyway.'

'Oh, so you aren't going to go to Seaside Park after all?'

'No. I probably misheard where I was meant to be going too, so once I go home and charge my phone I can check with my friend where we're meeting. Either way I can't use this phone, so even if I go to Seaside Park, there's a good chance I won't be able to contact my friend when I get there. And, besides, I still don't know which Seaside Park to go to.'

'Ah, I am so sorry, Miss. If I hadn't borrowed your phone, you could have used it to call your friend.'

That's fine, I said. I told the driver to take us to Sunshine City Aquarium for the time being and I'd get out there. The driver looked relieved, started the meter and set off.

'Ah, but you see you really helped me out there, Miss, lending me your phone like that.'

'It's not a big deal. If the driver hadn't asked, I wouldn't have known there were several Seaside Parks either.'

'Er, yes, I had to check because if I made a mistake with a customer's destination, I'd get a right telling off, wouldn't I?' the taxi driver said, sounding confused.

'Ah, that reminds me... You know, lately, I've just been hooked on goya champuru!'[13]

After Kaizu's abrupt comment he saw me tilt my head and wrinkle my brow in confusion and so he repeated the word 'goya.'

'Did you say 'goya'?'

'Yes, that's right. The dish from Okinawa. Lately I've just felt like making delicious goya champuru, so I've had it for about a week straight. Goya champuru every meal. It's good stuff, goya. It's a bitter vegetable, with a rich taste, but most importantly, it's good for your health. Right? You can taste the healthiness!'

'Is that so? That's nice to see, a man who can cook.'

'Oh no, it's only since I separated from my wife. I've

---

13. An Okinawan stir fry dish containing bitter melon, tofu, egg and meat.

been cooking for myself, doing the dishes and the laundry too. Well, I'm doing it all without help from anyone. It's the first time I've been impressed with what a capable person I turned out to be at this age. You see, it's not that me and my wife had a particular falling out. We didn't have a fight or fall out of love. It was simply being together for twenty years. We started having these conversations. 'Isn't it enough that we've already been together all this time?' we'd say. 'Wouldn't we be better off apart?' Take cornflakes. If you pour milk over them and leave them to stand for just five minutes, they go soggy, don't they? So what do you think would happen if the cornflakes and milk were left soaking in a bowl together for 20 years? Well, as you can imagine, it would be terrible. Do you understand? Living together for twenty years is a considerable feat. In that time, a child would go from a baby to 20 years old. Do you understand? There weren't any children for us, so, well, that may be why... You see, maybe the fact that we don't have children means that the cornflakes and the milk can separate. Because, yes, look, if you put raisins in or something, it'd no longer be possible for them to part ways, if only cornflakes and the milk wanted to, would it? All three would form a holy cereal trinity, and there would be a new flavour there. If the cornflakes and milk separated, the raisins would have to follow one of them, and that would be terrible. Take cornflakes and raisins, say, or milk and raisins. That wouldn't be tasty at all, would it? There'd be no sense pairing them up, would there? In our case, though, it's just the two of us, so it was simple. *Maybe we should split up soon,* we thought. *We'll soon be coming up to 20 years together.* We loved each other, we still love each other, so sometimes we'll meet up at Sunshine City Aquarium or the Ghibli Museum. I guess that makes me a bit strange! For some reason those are the kinds of places I'm always inviting her to. It's been like that ever since we started courting. Do you know, for our first date we rode on an elephant? An outrageous woman, honestly. We still meet in the same kinds of places, have some idle conversation, talk about how I'm hooked on goya champuru, and then sometimes we'll have sex or sometimes we won't, and then we'll part with a 'See you later'. Well, when you reach this age, there are often times when you can't get it up. 'And you used to be so impressive, didn't you?' she'll tell me. But hearing that kind of thing makes it even more difficult to get it up. Perhaps my ex-wife knows this and that's why she says it. What's a man to do in that situation? But, you know, by now I've got completely fine with hearing those kinds of things. If I'd been told all this when I was a younger man, though, I think I'd have killed my ex-wife already. And there's no way I could've had this conversation with a young woman back then. I couldn't stand these kinds of conversations when I was younger. But now it's fine. That's because, well, you could say I've "wilted". As a man, that is.'

'I've been sexless lately,' I replied. 'I haven't had sex with my boyfriend for two months. It's been three years since we started dating. But I think it's different to being married for twenty years and getting a divorce like you. We haven't even made it to marriage. Since about a year after we started dating, the sex has got gradually less and less frequent, so now it happens about once a month. And the thing is, it's somehow mechanical. Yes, the sex has become mechanical. It feels as if we've become this machine that only carries out simple, repetitive tasks. It's like there's no opening or closing act. What are those disposable vaginas called, an Onacup? No, is that right? Having sex with me is the same as with one of those masturbation devices. I'm on autopilot. My hips are something to pound with. So what I'm saying is, maybe that's the kind of woman I am, and so masturbation might be better than sex. Simpler. If I had to choose one, that is. If we're only doing it once a month, wouldn't it be better not having sex at all? That's what I think. And why once a month? Isn't that a strange routine? Wouldn't it just be less bother to not have sex at all? Even though I'm with my boyfriend, I think about all the different men I broke up with, or left for him, before we got together, only a few years ago, and I think, *Give me back those men!* Do you think there's anything strange about what I'm saying?'

'The thing is, Miss, that cycle you're in is fine when you're young. But I don't think you'll have more regular sex as time goes on. That's men for you. There are times, somehow or other, when things can get back on track, but you can't go back to the way you felt then. Because that's men for you. Am I right, driver?'

The taxi driver looked uncomfortable at being suddenly pulled into the conversation. He tilted his head and offered a vague reply of 'Huh? Hmm, well... I wonder.'

I didn't know why I had told him those things, but I realised that I felt some sort of hope. I was expecting something from him. He could do something to save my sexual desire, I thought.

'Yes. It's true. Of course young men are no good. The only thing that's strong is their pride. Yes, the age-old problem. If things go well, they can stay on course. But the thing with men, you see, is they're like an airplane trail. Do you understand? An airplane trail isn't an airplane is it? It's a cloud of vapour. Without substance. I wonder whether men are the same sort of formless things. Imagine if semen with tens of thousands of sperm gets squirted onto the ground in the shape of a human body. You know, like that white tape that marks a dead body in a crime scene. I think that is what men are like – men are just these hollow entities. We are just a shape inside this white tape, men are. And so if you think about it like that, well, it's all absurd, isn't it? I mean, worrying over this and that about men. This is what men are like. Animal males, though, I think they're different again. They hunt, and they create lots of offspring. That's why someone like me with no children ends up with a lot of things to think about. Whether I want to or not. But you're still young, Miss, so there should be plenty of men out there, right? That's an advantage. One of many advantages of youth. An advantage.

You have all sorts of options. Men, however, they'll always be alone. Even if they have a wife or a kid, they're by themselves, essentially. And this is unbearable. I guess that's what they call "the lightness of unbearable being," or something, isn't it? This must all sound very silly from a woman's point of view. But I've been thinking the same thing lately. You know, maybe being alone is fine. Because I think I'm slightly different now, compared to who I was when I'd cry "Men are alone!". It's probably that, yes. It's probably because I can't really get it up anymore. I'm no longer a man.'

I suddenly realised that I was not imagining having sex with Kaizu. And when I raised my hands to my breasts, I realised they didn't feel especially different to how they had before. Had I always been an E cup? And had there been a boyfriend who liked video games, who I'd been dating for three years? How far had my sexual desire wandered alone? And what had I been trying to do by letting it run wild? My adorable desire. Instead, I should fix my desire with a ribbon, strap on a collar and take it for a walk – but it is uncontrollable. I want the two of us to date on friendly terms, and come together with mutual affection and to love one another, and sleep in the same bed and have sex, but we don't understand each other. No matter how long we're together or where we go, that game of hating each other and using each other will continue. I think we'll break up eventually. I wonder if then I'd be able to be myself? Separated from my desire, I'd no longer be me, and I wouldn't be a new me, or a revolutionised me, or a me who had shed her skin. If I was split from my sexual desire I am sure that, in that moment, the person I am would vanish.

'You should come over for goya champuru some time!' Kaizu's offer brought me back to reality. When he got out of the taxi, I waved at him, then faced forward. After telling the driver the name of a park near my home, I closed my eyes. The taxi driver didn't answer. Inside, the cab was perfectly still. I wondered at that moment if it was possible that I was not actually in a taxi at all, but elsewhere. But I didn't open my eyes. *Oh, Mambo.* This silly phrase repeated inside my head, over and over again. Why would a song like this be there, I wondered, and then I recalled that 'Mambo' was one of the words Kaizu had said.

Vortex

Osamu Hashimoto

Translated by Asa Yoneda

I

A SMALL CHICKWEED WAS peeking out of a corner of the garden flowerbed. It was short, but flowering already. *I only just weeded,* thought Masako, and uprooted it. Even though it was hardly going to do much harm if she let it be.

Masako doesn't know the name of this plant she pulls up. She only thinks of it as *one of the weeds that grow in the garden*, and pulls it out as soon as she spots one. Of the weeds that sprout in the garden, shepherd's purse is the only one whose name she knows. When Masako finds it among the weeds in the garden, she thinks, *Oh, that's shepherd's purse.* She thinks that, but then pulls it up anyway, the tall and slender plant that's on the verge of dancing, with its white flowers like snow. But she doesn't know chickweed's name.

It shows up along with other weeds beside the bricks that form the border of the flowerbed. When it first peeks out, it's clearly a weed, but left to grow undisturbed it gets to about four inches tall, and might be taken for a small but nonetheless flowering plant – she's done it before. For a weed, it's not very weedy. Unlike the solitary shepherd's purse, it sends up multiple stalks, and puts out leaves, and small white flowers. Its leaves and stalks are a soft-looking light-green colour, and it uproots easily when pulled. It seems to be lacking in the tenacity so characteristic of weeds.

Once, when she accidentally left one to grow in the

corner of the garden, it got to a height of about eight inches and spread out like the crown of a wild herb which wouldn't have looked out of place in a salad. When she said, 'I wonder if it's edible,' to her daughter, who was still in elementary school at the time, her daughter said, 'Of course not, Mum.' But this was a long time ago.

The spring light had been gentle. It had made it seem like the unknown weed belonged in that spring day. And though flowers of all colours adorned the flowerbed, she had gazed at the weed with its small white flowers, thinking, *What is this plant?* It had seemed somehow familiar. But the house that Masako had grown up in had had no sunlit garden. Its modest garden was separated from the road outside by a slatted fence which put most of it in shadow.

She'd searched her memory, but come up empty-handed. *Maybe I'm mistaken*, she'd thought, and pulled up the plant that had grown in the garden, and stayed crouched there, lost in thought. There were more weeds in front of her, and the warm spring sun was on her back.

She must have had her hands full back then, with a young and growing child, but even then she'd got lost in thought, weeding the garden. She hadn't thought it *fulfilling* to be occupied, or *comfortable* to be able to afford to let time slip by.

With a growing child around, a house gets cluttered. It seemed like confusion spread through the house as the child grew. In the morning, her daughter would shout 'Mu–m, where is it?' and she'd reply, 'Where's what?', skirmishing with her daughter before school. By the time she'd set off, her room would be strewn with clothes already, and she'd think, *How did that happen?*

Masako would say 'Tidy your room!' only to do it herself, and clean, and do the washing, without ever stopping to think about it. She had to; otherwise, the house would be overrun by something, like an unweeded garden. *I couldn't sort it all out if I tried*, she thought, which made her anxious – it wasn't unbearable, but somehow, she didn't feel at ease. That restlessness had become normal, and some part of her had given up on getting everything in order.

But her daughter was married now, and the house was tidy. With no one to clutter it, everything was still and silent. The only living, growing things were the weeds in the garden. Without a young person around, it felt like there was a void in the house.

When her daughter, who by then was already working, said she wanted to rent a room and live on her own, her husband pulled an inscrutable expression. He'd never been the one to scold their daughter. 'Please, can't I?' she said, well aware of that. 'Commuting is so tough,' she said, and looked tired.

It was obvious her husband didn't want to let his daughter go. He was trying to abstain from the decision, and leave everything up to his wife. He would hardly want to say something that would turn her against him.

'Masako? What do you think?' he asked, addressing her much more politely than usual.

When Masako said, 'If that's what she wants, there's nothing I can do,' her daughter said 'Cheers!', and left the table.

It wasn't like anyone had actually made the call. Something unavoidable had come up, and there was *nothing to be done.* The time came for her child to say, 'I want to live on my own', just as the time had once come for her to start school. She didn't know whether there was a clear reason why her daughter needed to live on her own. Her daughter was now 25, and *a working woman.* She got home late. Masako wondered whether her daughter, who found commuting tough, wouldn't find it even more difficult to be on her own, but in as much as she'd said she wanted to move out, all Masako could tell herself was, *There's nothing I can do.*

That night, in the dark, in the bedroom, her husband said from under the covers, 'Hey–'. When Masako said,

'What?', there was a silence, and then he said, 'Never mind.' He didn't say anything after that. *Never mind what?* thought Masako.

Her husband was indecisive. He didn't know when to let things go. She thought about that, instead of about her daughter leaving home. Since her husband had laid claim to the feelings she might have had, there was nothing left for her but to be placid.

And so her daughter went. And from the flat she rented, she went to be someone's wife. While her daughter was single and living on her own, Masako could say 'Come back home once in a while', when they spoke on the phone. Now that she was married, she could hardly say that any more. She thought that the house had filled with a melancholy shadow since she'd agreed to let her daughter move out. She'd assumed it would pass, but her daughter was already some stranger's wife, with a different name. There was nothing to regret. Still, at times, she found herself letting out a breath she didn't know she'd been holding.

Masako laid the small chickweed she'd uprooted on the sunny bricks of the flowerbed, as if to preserve it by drying it, and went inside. The garden soil was dark, with the green of the weeds gone.

The house was dark inside. She could feel the bright light from outside enveloping her in the doorway like a halo. Unexpectedly, Masako thought of her mother.

Masako had two brothers, the eldest six years older than her, and the second four years older. As kids, her two brothers would often go out to play together. The elder one would set off somewhere, and the younger would follow. Her mother would call out each time, 'Take Masako, too.' As if those words were a signal, Masako would run outside, shouting, 'Wait for me–!', but her infant legs were no match for her brothers, who were already in their fourth and sixth years of school by this point. They were never interested in letting their much younger sister tag along.

On one occasion, when Masako came back, having lost sight of her brothers, she found her mother inside, sitting in the room behind the closed paper screen-doors. When she climbed up onto the veranda outside the room, which was bathed in sunlight, and slid open the doors, saying, 'Mum,' the room inside was dark. She saw her mother sitting there.

II

Masako was a woman without distinguishing features. Since getting married, she'd been a stay-at-home wife, and until then she'd been an 'Office Lady'. She wasn't one of these 'OL's who dreamed of marriage, nor an 'OL' who lived for her career, nor one who aspired to balance work and married life.

She finished junior college and got a job, assuming she'd resign when she got married. Neither doubting nor believing in the future, she thought of the word *future* itself as something that described society, not anything to do with her. *Tomorrow* always arrived; it wasn't a question of believing. If she thought about anything, all she thought was that there was no need for her to think of bothersome things. She felt no need to dwell on things that she didn't need to think about.

She didn't dislike school, nor did she like it. Studying in preparation for the entrance exams for high school, and then junior college, she'd thought: *I'm not cut out for this.* Afterwards, she assumed the exams had been the last of those tiresome obligations one had to fulfil before getting started on life.

After that, things followed their proper course. Each day arrived as expected. No reason to doubt. No need to aim especially high. The thing called *society* continued its steady, gentle rise, lifting up Masako and the whole of Japan. There was no reason to be particularly ambitious, nor any need for questions. Regardless of whether you ended up possessing them or not, desirable things presented themselves of their own accord, if you only waited a while. It was that kind of time. Masako might have lacked any distinguishing features, but that was never a disadvantage for her. Featureless, Masako was average, and normal. Young women shone simply by virtue of being young women.

So Masako has never doubted herself. Why should she need to? Being normal was a perfectly admirable virtue.

They called the time she grew up in *a period of rapid growth*. A time of dizzying progress and a miraculous recovery from the devastation of the war – she thought it must have been, since they said so. But Masako didn't understand what made one time different from another. She'd never seen any bombed-out ruins from the war, or even anything that made her think that there had ever been a war in Japan. When she was very young, she overheard her mother saying to someone, 'Times were tough, back then!' and asked her, 'How come?' Her mother said, 'There was a war. There were incendiaries, and all sorts of terrible things.' Masako said, 'What's incendiaries?'

They called it a miraculous reconstruction, so it must have been. But Masako didn't think that the age she'd grown up in was especially miraculous. She felt that as she had grown, the age, too, had progressed apace, and unfolded according to schedule. She came to think this way just as she was getting used to hearing the term *rapid growth* from all the retrospective television programmes which were broadcast when the Showa era ended, and then again at the turn of the century.

Rapid growth sounded almost like a time when high rise buildings would appear out of the ground before your eyes, like bamboo shoots pushing their way out of the earth in time-lapse photography. And indeed, there were television programmes about the period which showed that very image, along with grainy black and white footage of hordes of people crowding down the stairs of train stations at rush hour. Masako didn't find them nostalgic. There was something odd about seeing a period she had lived through appear on the screen in monochrome. Seeing the degraded and fading footage of the Osaka World Expo, she thought *Of course, I was there,* but it felt distant from her, lacking in excitement.

Watching clips of the crowds thronging the Expo, she suddenly recalled the bustle of the pedestrian promenade in Ginza, which she'd visited with friends when she was in high school.

The Expo had been a family trip, with her parents and two elder brothers. It must have been during the summer vacation. It was crowded and uncomfortable. And although they'd made the visit, the experience never came up afterward as a topic of conversation in the family. The family she knew were quiet and restrained. So when her eldest brother, who was at university, started some kind of argument with their father, and her other brother, who was in high school, took his brother's side, she was surprised. Something had happened without her noticing, had transformed her brothers and driven them to shouting, and she was afraid. Her mother retreated wordlessly to the kitchen, and silently wiped down the sink and surfaces. Thinking her mother must know something, she said, 'What's going on?' But her mother stayed silent and said nothing.

With a family like that, perhaps it was no wonder that Masako hadn't particularly enjoyed going to the Expo and spending time with them standing in the packed crowd. It must have been around the same time that she'd gone to the Ginza pedestrian zone for the first time, but that felt like something that belonged to a different timeline – the memory resurfaced vividly whenever she thought about it. They'd gone as a group of three boys and two girls who were in the same class at school, and she'd felt bright and free.

She knew there had been three boys, but couldn't now recall who they were. Certainly, her secret crush hadn't been among them. She came to take the pedestrian zone for granted before long, but as for any teenage girl, her first encounter with it was special. All it was was people walking in the road, between the buildings on either side, but the sky felt bright and big, and she looked around her and thought, *Ginza's pretty*.

The house she grew up in stood in a nondescript residential area crowded with wooden houses, of a kind found anywhere in Tokyo. The single-storey, timber-framed house held her parents, her two elder brothers, and, until she was in middle school, her paternal grandfather. Tokyo itself wasn't an especially fashionable location yet, just a town where people lived, not very different from the other, regional cities of Japan. Because the residential areas made up a relatively large proportion of it, its character as a city was somewhat vague. Tokyo was just Tokyo, and it neither had any noteworthy features nor posed any special hardships. A *miraculous transformation* might have been taking place, somewhere, but it was the sort of thing that happened outside of the world a child could know.

For the young Masako, Tokyo was the town that contained the house she lived in, and there was no need for it to be anything more. That town might have undergone changes of its own as Masako grew up, but she never thought of it that way. It seemed to her that new areas of the city became visible each time she stepped forward into a new phase of life. This thought occurred to her when she graduated from her local middle school, and started taking the train every day to her high school.

The rush hour crush of her commute was bad, but finding herself getting the train at that time, just as her father and brothers did, she suddenly thought, *I've grown up*. She thought that growing up was being able to go places on one's own, expanding the scope of one's movements. As she stepped forward into adulthood, she felt that the town of Tokyo was blossoming apace with her progress. The town was newly peaceful. It had lost the prickliness she'd felt while in elementary school and middle school, and felt calm, like sailing a still sea. Her eldest brother, who had got a job, and her second brother, who was at university, no longer spoke to their father with raised voices. They didn't argue, but were somehow stand-offish with him – or rather, they kept their distance. To Masako, it seemed only natural that they should do this, now that they were grown up.

It seemed that all of a sudden, there were three grown men in the house, which had never been spacious to begin with. Mealtimes were cramped, with the three men and two women, Masako and her mother, eating at the low table set up on the tatami mats. There wasn't much conversation. Even so, when her brothers were late to the evening meal, it felt like there was something missing. When she asked her father, who was already at the table, where they were, he stayed silent, his head at a slight angle. Her elder brother was by then a working member of society, and was routinely late, as if that was only to be expected. Her second brother, who was at university, came home late, too, as though to follow his lead. Masako found herself contemplating the night-time city that contained her brothers.

She and her brothers got on well enough. But the two of them, being close in age, treated their much younger sister like a child, and spoke to her only of trivial things. Those same brothers were now grown, and turned up late to evening meals at their mother's table as though it was their prerogative. Their father, who worked for a small accounting firm, watched TV nearby without saying a word. Having put two sons into university, he didn't have the means to extend the house. With both grown brothers at home, the house felt crowded. Masako, in high school now, was no longer a child, either. Not realising it yet, she only thought, *Something's changed,* but had no way of processing that idea. It wasn't yet a time when children looked forward to leaving home and living on their own. In Tokyo, with schools and offices close by, there was no need to even consider it.

Masako never wondered why her brothers didn't move out. Nor did it occur to her that she might do so herself. It was only much later, when her daughter grew up and said she wanted to live on her own, that it dawned on Masako that she'd never had such a choice.

Time passed as expected, and she passed the time without questioning it, only noticing it once it had passed.

She noticed, and grasped at it, but her outstretched hand never reached. The media kept looking back on that time in recent history as a *period of rapid growth*, but Masako had no real understanding of what they meant. Once she'd left home and started *making her own way,* she was marking time within herself, and her connection to the society she lived in gradually faded.

III

Looking back, the past is indistinct. She's not even trying to look back, but images of the past come at her through the television, and when she tries to recall those times within herself, there's nothing there. It's all vague, and she can't make out anything from that time – she must have been somewhere, doing something, but she can't recall what. Things get clearer after she's had a child, but the time between starting college and getting married is a blur. *Why does everything feel so hazy?* she thinks, feeling compelled to look back into the formless past without knowing why. Then she sees her mother, sitting alone in a dark room.

When she hauled herself up on to the veranda and slid open the paper door, her mother was sitting at a low table, operating the knitting machine. Masako had known she was there even before opening the door, because she'd heard the rhythmic, crunching sound of the knitting machine carriage moving across the needles. Her mother made some money making jumpers on the machine for people in the neighbourhood.

Her work was neat. Masako liked wearing jumpers her mother had knitted for her, although her brothers didn't.

She went into the room and sat down near her, and said 'Mum,' and her mother said 'What?' Having answered, she carried on moving the knitting machine's handle from side to side. When she moved the handle, it made a zipping sound, and – apparently – knitted another row on the jumper, though Masako, watching at her side, couldn't see any change. There was a television in the corner of the room. There was nothing broadcast in the afternoon, and she was forbidden even to switch it on. There was nothing else to watch, so she watched her mother's hands at work. Then she heard her grandfather call out from the back room.

Her mother said 'Yes,' without slowing her hands which were moving the handle. Still working, she said 'Go see what grandpa wants.' Masako's grandfather, who was retired, lived with them, and would still have been in good health at that time, although she didn't know what he did all day. Grandpa was just Grandpa. He just lived at home, and sometimes pottered in the garden, tending to the things he'd planted. That was all. Her mother looked after him. He must have had a wife once, her mother's mother-in-law, but she was dead by then, and Masako has no memory of her.

Masako's mother died toward the end of the 20th century. She had just celebrated her *kiju*, her 77th year, when she died, leaving behind her husband, who was 82. Masako's father was in the same position as her grandfather had been, but he lived on his own despite his age, without anyone looking after him. At the ceremony that marked 49 days after her passing, Masako wondered about the grandmother she must have had.

'Do you remember Grandma?' she asked her eldest brother. Her brother, who was past 50 by then, said 'Yeah.' That was all. 'What about you?' she asked her second brother, who said, 'I remember her being there – I think, but I'm not really sure.'

'What about you?' he asked Masako.

'I never knew her,' she said. 'Only from the photo on the shrine at home.'

Her daughter, Rie, who was in high school, said 'You had a grandma?'

'Granny died the year you were born, or thereabouts, that's why you don't remember her,' her eldest brother said to

Masako, and asked their father, 'What was she like?'

'You don't remember her either?' said Masako.

'I remember she was there, but I don't know – was she in hospital?' said her eldest brother.

Their father, asked about his mother, said '62. Died at 62.' This was long before he started losing his memory, but that was all he said. Perhaps there came a point, after someone died, when you stopped speaking of them except in numbers.

Masako wondered what her dead mother had thought. She'd sat in a gloomy room working at her knitting machine, and looked after Masako's grandfather, who did nothing in particular. As a child, Masako could never have asked 'Mum, are you happy?' She lived in the old house with her husband even after her sons had married and left home, just the two of them, and never found much to complain about. Her daughters-in-law, about whom she might otherwise have complained, lived elsewhere.

The year Masako was 22, her eldest brother got married. There'd been plans to extend the house at the same time, but they got shelved. When Masako said 'Why?' her mother said in a low voice, 'Takiko is against it.'

The woman who was going to be her brother's wife was refusing to live with her in-laws. *It's only natural*, Masako thought. Living there meant not only living with his parents, but also his younger, unmarried siblings. If her brother's wife had said, 'I don't want to move in to such a crowded house,' then Masako would have thought it only fair. That said, she couldn't wholeheartedly welcome her brother's soon-to-be wife, who made her mother have to lower her voice and say 'I gather that Takiko...' The woman who was marrying her brother was the first outsider to join their family. Masako, at 22, secretly thought *It's for the best that she doesn't want to live with us.* You could choose your friends, but you couldn't choose your sister-in-law.

She neither liked nor disliked her; the woman who married her brother was just there, as her brother's wife. They saw each other sometimes, but that was no reason to feel anything. Masako, who was by then an 'OL', knew how to get along with others. There was no need to get close to them just for the sake of it. All you had to do was avoid giving the other person any reason to dislike you – this was Masako's view, but it was different for her mother.

Masako's mother started showing a different side of herself around the time her eldest son got engaged. At first, Masako thought, *She probably doesn't like his choice of wife,* but she couldn't think of a reason why that should be. His fiancée, Takiko, wasn't especially objectionable or unlikeable. Masako just thought *So that's the kind of person he's going to marry*, and that was all there was to it. She felt a far more definite dislike for the wife of Tsuguo, her second brother, who married a year before she did.

Tsuguo's wife was strong-willed, and looked it. She would look at Masako, who was nearly the same age, as though to appraise her. She was obviously proud of the fact that she'd gone to a university, and even ordered Tsuguo around. When Masako said, 'What do you think, mum? She...' looking for agreement, to her surprise her mother said, 'That's just how it is. Tsuguo likes it that way.' It obviously didn't matter to her what her second son's wife was like.

Takiko, the wife of Masako's eldest brother, Shōtaro, wasn't especially pretty. She had a nondescript, ordinary face. But in that respect Masako was similar, and Takiko was never overtly unkind, despite having refused, in secret, to live with them. She was an unremarkable conversationalist, and that seemed to rub Masako's mother up the wrong way, but it shocked Masako to hear her complain about her eldest son's wife. She found it difficult to believe that her own mother would say such spiteful things about another person. *Where had this side of her been hiding, all these years?* Masako wondered, and realised something: her mother didn't like her eldest son's wife because she had special feelings toward her eldest son. Masako thought this must be it, and was puzzled.

It had never occurred to Masako that her mother might harbour strong feelings of love somewhere within her. Her mother was gentle and calm with everyone, and didn't seem the type to take sides. She didn't play favourites with Masako and her brothers, but if she did have a favourite, Masako thought it would be her, since she was her youngest, and a daughter. She didn't seem to be especially affectionate to her eldest, and was always nagging him about something or other. In fact, she'd never seemed to be a person who used affection as a way of expressing love – not that she was ever stern with Masako.

She'd once told her, 'You were the baby girl we'd always wanted.' That was how she expressed love, and Masako felt pride at those words. But she hadn't sensed any stronger emotion lying beneath them. Her mother loved her firstborn son especially, and Masako had had no idea.

She wasn't especially taken aback by the realisation. She felt somehow validated to learn that passionate feelings lay dormant within her mother.

Masako was 25 when her second brother got married. She wasn't yet engaged. It had been five years since she graduated from junior college and started work, assuming she'd get married *in due course*. The sense of *in due course* made her pass the time idly, and it wasn't that she didn't date in that time, but while she was young, so were the people she dated. They never got as far as thinking about marriage, and by the time she realised it had been five years, Masako was beginning to feel frustrated. She felt strong emotions within herself she couldn't entirely control, and so her mother's strong feelings made sense to her, too.

For a while, mother and daughter each bore their own, separate frustrations, but then the eldest son's wife gave birth to the firstborn grandchild, a boy. Masako's mother, who had been critical of everything throughout the pregnancy, had nothing more to say; she was too busy being affectionate to her grandchild to nag at her daughter-in-law. She suddenly started travelling to where her son and daughter-in-law lived, to see her grandchild, which she'd rarely done before.

Around the same time, Masako received a marriage proposal from a colleague who'd joined the company the same year she did. Although they'd started at the same time, he was a graduate of a four-year college, and so was two years older.

Masako's greatest fear – and the reason for her frustration – was *falling behind the times*. She'd never been left behind by anything before. She'd kept herself from aiming too high just to avoid it. She had no major complaints. But once she passed 25, she was assaulted by a mysterious anxiety. She couldn't do anything about it on her own. But nor could she ask anyone to get rid of it for her. Her pride said, *This is a problem I should be able to deal with on my own, it's not something worth worrying over.* That kept her from talking about it, which increased her frustration. Then someone came along and proposed. It was as though the blossoms of a cherry tree at the height of its flowering had fallen in a flash, and been replaced by the new green leaves of early summer. There was nothing at all to worry about.

Once the eldest son had married and set up his own household, and the second son had left the same way, too, it was only natural that the youngest daughter should marry and move out as well. Masako thought of her parents being left alone in the house, and wondered aloud to the man she was going to marry: 'I hope they'll be all right.' The man she was going to marry was called Nakazawa, and was originally from the provinces. His parents back home already lived alone with their elderly parents.

Hearing Masako wonder, Nakazawa asked her, 'Don't you think they will?' Masako had no way of answering. 'I'm sure they'll be fine,' she said.

Finding themselves living in a time of abundance and prosperity, they never thought about *having their hands so full living their own lives that they had no time to think of others*. It never occurred to them to think that way.

After saying goodbye to Nakazawa, Masako came home and sat down in front of her father, who was watching television, and said, 'Father.' She didn't feel she could speak to him alone, so she craned her neck and called to her mother, who was in the kitchen. 'Mother.'

Her mother came out drying her hands on her apron, saying, 'Yes, dear?' but then quickly sensed something was up, and took off her apron and sat down.

Her mother was sitting up straight. Her father put down the cigarette he was smoking, and sat up a little, too. A curl of blue smoke rose from the ashtray, and her mother told her husband, 'Put that out.'

Her father stubbed out the cigarette, and her mother said, 'The television, too.' Her father reached out to turn the television off, and her mother relaxed her posture slightly as he did.

Father and mother looked to their daughter in silence. Masako said, 'If I get married, will the two of you be all right on your own?'

Her father replied in a firm voice that she hadn't often heard him use. 'We'll be fine. Don't worry about us.' This was toward the very end of the time when parents had the habit of taking that kind of distant tone toward their children when saying something particularly parental.

Her mother said, 'You don't worry about us, and take good care of Mr. Nakazawa,' and her father nodded and said, 'That's right.'

Masako only said, 'Okay,' rather than, 'I will.' It wasn't yet time to bow deeply to her parents and say, 'Thank you for bringing me up.' And Masako never did. In her wedding dress in the dressing room at the wedding venue, she only said, 'Here I go, then.' She felt embarrassed to be any more formal in front of her brothers and their wives.

IV

True to his word, her father carried on living alone even after her mother died, and died five years after his wife at the age of 87. For the last six months or so he was in and out of hospital, but until then he was hale and self-sufficient. She didn't know what it was that sustained him, but when she went back to the house to check on him, more and more often he'd say, 'Oh, I'm fine. Just fine.'

Her father liked to read. He seemed to enjoy it even more in his old age, and carried on frequenting bookshops, despite his habit of saying, 'They don't write them like they used to.' He didn't mind his married daughter coming to see him, but he seemed to be fine on his own. He might even have preferred it. When she said, 'But you must be a little lonely,' to her father, who seemed to have got used to being alone, he said, 'Well.' *He does feel it, after all,* thought Masako, but when she said, 'Dad, why don't you come and live with us?' he held out one hand, and waved it from side to side. It's not that he doesn't want to live with us, thought Masako. He just doesn't want to have to change the way he lives.

Once or twice a week, Masako would cook something at home and take it over to her father's. She'd started doing it while her mother was still alive, and her father was caring for her. At first, he would say 'Sorry to trouble you,' but after a while, when he'd been alone for some time, he started to say, 'Ah, thanks. Thanks.' It felt like the first sign of humanity she had seen in a long time from her father, who'd seemed to reject others in his desire to be himself, and she was glad of it.

Usually, he reheated the food in the microwave on his own, but when Masako did it for him and served him his meal, he said, 'Ah, you remind me of your mother.' *Of course, he does miss her,* thought Masako, and was glad to have recalled her to him. She felt an obscure sense of comfort.

Then her father died on his hospital bed, still wearing an oxygen mask. There might have been a quiver in his throat just before he died, but he died without any last words. When Masako squeezed his veiny hand as he lay dying, it was warm, but he didn't squeeze back.

Masako stood beside the hospital bed as if she were the sole blood relative, saying, 'Dad, dad!' while her brothers and their wives stood behind the youngest daughter of the family. When she turned around, her eldest brother's face was bereft of all expression. *Dad's really gone*, she thought.

After her father died, everything slowly disappeared. When her mother died, her daughter Rie had still been in high school. When her father died, Rie had finished university and was working.

Masako's daughter, who was in the cheerleading team at her high school, was a spirited girl. She thought nothing of telling her mother all about the boys in her class. Realising that her sweet young child had somehow turned into one of *today's young women*, Masako was surprised. She was surprised, then she got used to it. She felt like there was something caught in her throat, but it was only a feeling, and she couldn't have said what the thing might have been.

It had simply started to dawn on her: *It wasn't like this for me.*

Without her noticing it, a distance had opened up between her and the world. The way her daughter was made that clear. Given that she could hardly go back to being young herself, there was no use thinking, *That's not how it used to be.* Understanding came more easily if she thought, *That's what girls are like these days.* When, in the face of the mystifying *up-to-date information* coming from the television, she asked her daughter, 'What is that?', her daughter only said, 'That? That's nothing special.'

'Oh…' thought Masako, taking it in. She didn't know how or where she came by it, but her daughter seemed to know everything.

That daughter had finished college, found a job, and was in attendance at her grandfather's funeral, wearing the black suit she had bought when she started job hunting.

Her daughter had landed a permanent position at a company in the food service industry. She worked hard, and was strong-willed. She'd got into university on a recommendation and carried on cheerleading, but in the summer of her second year, she came back from the team's training camp and said, 'I'm going to quit.' When Masako said 'Why?', she only said, 'It's too stressful.'

When Masako said, 'What's stressful?' she said, 'The interpersonal stuff.' But when Masako asked, 'How so?', she wouldn't elaborate. 'It just is!' she said, and left the room.

Seeing her daughter's intractability, Masako said, 'I wonder who she takes after? Dad, I guess,' thinking of the way he'd insisted on living on his own. But her husband simply said, 'It's you.'

'I'm not that headstrong,' said Masako, and her husband said, 'Do you think so?' and smiled a little.

'When am I ever that pig-headed?' she pressed, and he said, 'My mistake, you're obviously nothing like that,' and turned to face the television, which was always on.

'No need to be rude,' said Masako, and then asked herself, silently – *But really, when?*

Masako thought of herself as someone who didn't make friends easily, and tended to withdraw from people. She wasn't wrong, but neither was that the whole of it.

V

Her hard-working daughter always came home exhausted. Often she got home late at night. Seeing the toll her job was taking on her, Masako said, 'Why don't you quit?' Her daughter said, 'Why should I?'

After a while, her daughter started phoning to say, 'I'll be staying at a business hotel tonight. I have to work late.'

When Masako said, 'Why do you have to work so hard? It's not as if you're a man,' all her daughter would say was, 'You just do.'

So when her daughter eventually said, 'I want to move out,' Masako thought, *I can't stop her. She won't quit her job, so there's nothing I can do.* Fleetingly, she thought, *Maybe she's got a man,* but since her daughter never mentioned it, she didn't dare ask.

Eventually her daughter got married, and there was nothing left for Masako to do. The evening that her daughter rang to say she was engaged, Masako suddenly saw her father's face, in profile, as she'd seen it when he lay dying. She didn't know why. She found it strange, too, that she couldn't recall what her mother had looked like when she died, although she'd been there to see it.

While her daughter had been living on her own, Masako had visited, wondering whether she was really all right, bringing frozen home-cooked meals like she'd done for her father.

At one point, her daughter suddenly became less welcoming of these visits. Masako never knew it was because she and the man she was seeing were having problems.

Masako had to find something to do. She'd become a mother, and fulfilled that duty, and had been a good daughter to her elderly father, too. She must also have been a wife, to her husband, but there was nothing remarkable about being a wife, so she didn't feel any particular satisfaction from that. It wasn't that things had cooled between them; from the very beginning they'd been limited by their expectations of married life, and that was hardly going to change now. They continued to relate to each other as mother and father of their child, rather than as husband and wife.

One Sunday, sometime after their daughter had left home, her husband unexpectedly said, 'Shall we go and see a film?' Masako said, 'All right. What's playing?' and tagged along.

She didn't find it uninteresting, but she didn't find it interesting, either. Afterwards, her husband only said, 'Shall we go?', and offered no comments. It wasn't the kind of film there was a lot to say about, so Masako didn't say anything, either. She was certain that she and her husband had some times gone out to the cinema in their younger days, but she had no recollection of it. Her husband, at least, was no longer young. It was no use thinking of him as he used to be. The husband who said, 'Shall we go for *soba*?' outside the cineplex was today's husband, and seemed to have no link to the past. Her daughter, to whom she used to tell stories that went, 'When we were young, your dad used to…', or 'Ever since we met, your dad always…', was no longer around. Now that there was no one to listen, the words didn't even take shape in her mind. Masako just said, 'All right,' and followed the husband who'd said, 'Shall we go for *soba*?' Masako said, 'Where are we going?', and her husband said, 'Where shall we go?'

Once her daughter had left home, time started to weigh heavily on her hands, and Masako joined a calligraphy course at the cultural education centre in the large building that contained the train station. I've reached the time of life when people encourage you to *find a hobby,* she thought. Just when she'd finally regained her equilibrium and could feel calm in her body again after her menopause.

When she rubbed the stick of ink on the inkstone and faced the white paper, her mind quietened. The smell of the ink was pleasant. It was soothing to know she could practise and improve herself without anyone interfering. But she didn't make as much progress in her calligraphy as she'd hoped. And then her daughter got married, not to the man she'd dated while at university, but to someone she'd met through work.

Her daughter was tall, and the man she married was slender and tall, too. He was obviously good-looking. *She's got high standards*, she thought. *I brought her up right.*

After the wedding ceremony and the reception, her daughter and her new husband went on to the after-party. Masako got home and thought, *That's a big weight off my shoulders.* She thought it, but said nothing. Her husband silently went to open the curtains in the room. Seeing her husband standing in front of the glass doors, beyond which she could see into the garden, Masako was moved to say, 'Would you like a cup of tea?' And her husband, looking uncharacteristically touched, said 'Please.'

How many more responsibilities did she have to put down? Each one left her with less to do.

After a while, Masako stopped going to the calligraphy class. There were cliques among the students. For a long time it hadn't bothered her, but once it did, it became intolerable. She couldn't stand the way certain students, who'd been in the class longer and thought themselves accomplished, held sway over the group and excluded the beginners. What had brought on this realisation was seeing other women her own age at the junior college reunion she'd gone to, after her daughter was married.

It was her first reunion in a while, but when Masako turned up in clothes that she thought would be *age-appropriate*, the others all said, 'Darling, what happened?' Those who'd known her when they were young looked her over from head to toe. They were all over 50, but the women surrounding her glittered. Their voices were aggressive, and for a moment Masako recalled her junior college days, in the distant past. At junior college, she had been careful to stay away from things she found distressing. Then she got a job, then got married, and since then she had felt no need to involve herself with anything that made her uncomfortable. If she found something unpleasant, she felt free to reject it. With a family to protect, she could easily dismiss distressing things.

When she'd been active in the Parent-Teacher

Association at her daughter's school, her days had been taken up by factional disputes. Women who worked didn't tend to give much time to the PTA, and yet they would always barge in with objections to things that had already been decided. Being at her junior college reunion reminded her of that.

'Have you heard about so-and-so?' they'd ask, giving the name of a classmate who had done well for herself. 'You remember Hasegawa, don't you? After we graduated she went to a four-year college, and then moved to the States. Said she wanted to work in translation. Guess what she does now – she's the wife of a professor at Columbia University!'

'Oh, really!' the others said, sounding impressed. But then they said 'She didn't used to be like that, don't you think?' and put her character on trial, condemning her behind her back. It wasn't getting rich that was the problem, it was the fact that she'd climbed the social ladder. Masako stood in the corner of the room with a glass in her hand, not saying anything.

VI

Once she quit calligraphy, there was nothing for Masako to do. She had a husband, and he went to work, and came home from work. His existence gave her certain responsibilities. But there was nothing else. Whatever she did, whatever she thought of doing, there was always the question: *What good would it do?* Her future looked vague and misty. When she asked herself, *What do I want to do?* the answer was shrouded and invisible. The more she wondered what she wanted to do, the more the not knowing weighed on her. What she didn't realise was that she'd never in her life done something because she *wanted* to. The things she needed to concern herself with had always presented themselves to her at the appropriate time. But there was no more to come. The future wasn't arriving. Her husband seemed to epitomise this stagnating future. But she wasn't driven to take aggressive action: *What can't be helped, can't be helped*, she thought. Hence, her apathy.

Suddenly, she thinks of her mother, sitting in the shady room, working at her knitting machine. Masako, having just come in, said, 'Mum, isn't it dark in here?' At least, she seems to recall saying that.

She doesn't know where this memory has suddenly come from, but the shadows she steps into, coming back into the house from the bright garden, bring the sight of her mother back to her. It's not as though she misses her. But for some reason, there she is, sitting before the young Masako, who's just climbed up into the room from the garden; there she is, looking the way she did when she was young.

Remembering her mother, Masako feels everything get swallowed up by that distant moment. She loses sight of the time she's lived through, and feels it all get sucked away into some kind of vortex.

She has no idea when they grew. There are new weeds in the garden she just weeded. *They can't have grown so quickly*, thinks Masako, having lost her sense of time already.

Not just in the sunny part of the garden, but in shady corners as well, the light green weed is growing, and even sporting small white flowers.

Stepping into the shade to pull them, Masako feels slightly dizzy, and thinks, *I know this plant*. She doesn't know its name. She seems to recall her brothers gathering it.

At home, they had a pair of birds. She thinks they had white breasts, and black and pale grey markings on the wings. Her grandfather kept them in an old cage, probably made of bamboo. She thinks they were called society finches. The birdcage hung in the veranda, and her brothers were sticking their fingers inside through the gaps in the cage, teasing the birds.

Masako couldn't reach the cage. When she said, 'Me

too!', her brothers lifted her up, but when she tried to stick her fingers in, one of them shook her body from side to side, saying, 'Poke! Poke!' When Masako said 'Nooo!', quaking, they laughed and put her down, and then ran off somewhere together.

The garden laid out by her grandfather wasn't much fun for children. After a while, her brothers came back with their hands full of plants. 'What's that?' asked Masako, and one of them said, '*Whatsitsname.*' 'It's for the finches,' he said, and approached the bird cage again, holding out the weeds.

'Are they eating it?' her second brother asked, and her eldest brother said, 'Yeah.'

When Masako said, 'Me too!', wanting to join in, they turned to her, but said nothing. They carried on pushing the plants through the gaps in the cage, feeding the birds.

It's the same plant, Masako thinks now, with her back to the sun, in the sunny garden at the start of summer.

Her brothers were always playing together. Sometimes they fought together. Their grandfather, the owner of the birdcage, treated them as if the two of them were his only grandchildren. When their mother said, 'Why don't you include Masako,' they only said, 'Don't wanna,' and went out to play. Left alone on the veranda, Masako swung her legs over the edge, and looked at the garden, thinking, *Which plants can I feed to the finches?*

The garden bounded by a slatted fence, neither wide nor particularly light, was devoid of weeds, thanks to her mother and her grandfather's weeding. She'd once angered her grandfather by carelessly uprooting something green. He got angry, but didn't tell her why. Her mother pointed at a plant like the one that Masako had pulled up, and said 'That one's not a weed.' Masako couldn't tell what was a *good plant* and what was a *bad plant*. Even if she could have gathered the right weeds, she couldn't have reached the cage to feed them to the birds like her brothers had. As she sat on the veranda, the birdcage swayed above Masako's head, out of reach.

Once, when she said, 'Mum, I want to feed the birds,' her mother said, 'They're your grandfather's, you mustn't bother them.'

With nothing to do, Masako sat on the veranda, and slid open the sun-lit paper doors. Her mother was inside, moving the handle on the knitting machine back and forth, making a rasping sound. When the young Masako said, 'Mum,' her mother, without turning to her, said, 'Yes, dear?'. Then a voice from inside the house said, 'Hey,' and her mother said, 'Go to Grandpa and see what he wants, sweetheart.'

Masako said, 'Okay.'

It wasn't that she missed her mother. She missed the child she'd been when she was beside her. Her brothers might have left her behind, but when she said, 'Mum,' her mother had listened.

She'd always given Masako *something to do*, and so had set Masako on her path of growth.

'Mum was there,' murmurs Masako, hesitantly. She tries again, clearer: 'Mum.' The path that seemed to have been swallowed up by the vortex seems to reappear, dimly.

She remembered being told, 'Mum's busy just now, so you play on your own for a bit, all right?'

Masako said, 'Okay.' *Maybe that was when my life started,* she thinks. When she looks at the bright sky, the bright sky is a void. *I guess I've got to start back at the beginning again.*

The Hut on the Roof

Hiromi Kawakami

Translated by Lucy Fraser

A FEW STEPS INSIDE the entrance to Uoharu, there's a single photograph pinned to the wall. It's a photograph of two Western men. Both are wearing dark suits and standing with their elbows on a round table top at chest-height. One of the men is lanky while the other has a short, solid build. They're not looking at each other, nor are their eyes directed at the camera; both gaze vaguely into the distance.

'That's quite an old photograph,' I said to Heizō-san, and he nodded.

'You know who that is, *okusan*?'

Heizō-san addresses all the female customers in his shop as *okusan* – 'Mrs'. When I had first moved in I got huffy at being called *okusan* this and *okusan* that every time I bought a saury or a horse mackerel and responded in clear, clipped tones that I was not married.

'Oh, that so,' Heizō-san answered with a baffled expression, then continued with, 'Sorry, *okusan*.'

I couldn't tell whether he was making fun of me or whether he was just a bit inconsiderate, so it was my turn to be baffled. Gradually, I came to learn that Heizō-san was neither making fun of me nor was he inconsiderate. He is simply lacking in tact, or perhaps he is someone whose way of being tactful is a bit warped – that's Heizō-san.

Uoharu is the fishmonger's that Heizō-san's father opened soon after the war.

'I went to university, so I s'pose instead of taking over the fishmonger's I could've got a job at a normal company, married someone from work, and then eventually retired got into bonsai trees or something, and taken it easy,' he said once, pouring himself a warmed sake at a counter seat in the Budō-ya. I listened without thinking much but now I sometimes recall those words.

I only really got chatting to Heizō-san after I became a regular at the Budō-ya. It's an appealing venue with unvarnished wood counters, about midway between an izakaya[14] and a simple restaurant, run by the owner and a girl who helps out, together with Ren-san the cook.

'Ren-san's cooking's good, isn't it?'

Heizō-san spoke to me after I'd come for drinks a number of times, and they were finally becoming somewhat accustomed to me.

'Yes,' I answered. 'Because of the good ingredients, I'd say.' The Budō-ya purchases its stock from Uoharu. I had seen Heizō-san bring Styrofoam boxes in through the back door a number of times.

'Exactly, exactly. They use fish from my shop, y'know,' he said happily.

I simply smiled and nodded, not letting the words *I know* cross my lips. After that, Heizō-san and I would often chat. When we first spoke, he didn't seem to realise I sometimes bought fish at Uoharu. Even though he was supposed to be running a business, apparently it wasn't in his nature to remember his customers' faces.

'For that, there's Gen,' Heizō-san said with a laugh. 'Me, I'm no good at remembering stuff, never pay attention, but Gen, yep.'

When he used the name 'Gen,' Heizō-san would squint as though slightly dazzled by something. I had no interest whatsoever in who this 'Gen' was, but I nodded my head appropriately and said, 'Oh yes.'

---

14. An informal Japanese drinking establishment that serves food to accompany the drinks.

The Uoharu shop occupies the entire ground floor of a small three-storey building. A low glass display shelf is arranged in an L-shape with three large silver refrigerators lined up at the back. Apart from Heizō-san, there's one young shop assistant who fillets the large fish, preserves the blue-backed types of fish that haven't sold, and so on. If you go around to the back of the building you can see several three-tiered blue netting shelves hanging from a thick cord across the outside wall. Horse mackerel and butterfish are split open and set on the netting shelves to dry overnight.

Most of the restaurants and pubs in the neighbourhood buy their fish wholesale from Uoharu. The shop will also put together a sashimi platter if you order it. Once I even saw the owner of the futon shop bring in a large Imari porcelain plate, about 50 centimetres in diameter.

'My kid's fiancé is bringing his parents to visit,' the futon-shop owner was saying happily.

'They're getting married, eh? Good news,' Heizō-san replied with easy grace, as he took the plate. When the futon-shop owner left, Heizō-san issued copious instructions to the young shop assistant.

'So, use a lot of the good red flesh from the tuna. Just a bit of squid will do it. Bream, and then let's splurge on the top-quality prawns. Garnish with plenty of wakame seaweed, too. After all, wakame was one of the traditional betrothal gifts, you know? Must be good luck or something, wakame. Damn, maybe that's not wakame, maybe it's konbu I'm thinking of...'

Come to think of it, was Heizō-san himself married? Or had he once been married? I wondered then, as I listened to the exchange. There were no female assistants at Uoharu.

There was a peculiar hut standing on the roof of the Uoharu building. It was neither a storage shed nor an extra room built onto the roof: the only word for it was 'hut.'

'It's such an elegant building, but that thing plonked right on top of it – it needs knocking down,' the lady from Yaoyoshi, the greengrocer's next to Uoharu, had once given her assessment.

This suburb is only 20 minutes by rail or subway from the city centre, so it's extremely convenient to have property here. New apartments, older flats, and individual houses are jumbled together. Perhaps due to the large population, there's a big supermarket and two medium-sized ones, and they all appear to be prospering. Even so, the small shops in the shopping street are putting up a good fight, and have avoided closing down.

'We're agile, that's why – we can turn on a sixpence, us owner-operated shops,' said the lady from the greengrocer's.

'Only the places that own their premises have survived,' the bloke from Torikatsu, the chicken shop on the other side of Uoharu, commented a little more harshly.

At Torikatsu, I always buy the giblets with the small yellow eggs attached.

'They look like egg-yolks – very pretty,' I said, pointing at the glass case when I went to buy some chicken roulade.

'They are eggs, and they're tasty, and this dish is easy to cook,' he explained. He told me you just stew it all in a soy-sauce-based broth, so I tentatively bought some and took it home. He was right, it was tasty. Not just the eggs – the gizzards I couldn't name, sticking to the eggs, were not pungent at all but flavoursome and tender.

'Explaining things like that, that's what I mean by agile,' the lady from the greengrocer's said, nodding plausibly.

'More importantly, what is that hut on the roof of Uoharu?' I tried asking.

'Ah, up over there. Gen-san lives up over there.'

That was the second time I heard the name 'Gen-san'. The third time I heard it, I met Gen-san himself. When I went to Uoharu one evening, a man emerged from out the back. He was an excessively tall elderly man. He was… how can I put it? He gave off an air of – that's it – austerity.

That man was Gen-san.

At the back of the Uoharu shop was a small room the size of about four and a half tatami mats, where the cooking implements were all assembled. I knew this, because I once sneaked a peek inside when Heizō-san was out. The young shop assistant didn't notice me peeking in, entirely absorbed as he was in wolfing down his bowl of rice. Further inside the four-and-a-half-mat room was a set of stairs. They were straight, steep stairs that appeared to lead to the second floor. Did that mean Heizō-san lived on the second floor? If so, there was no sign of his family. Perhaps Heizō-san was alone in the world. I retreated outside to think over the possibilities.

Had Gen-san come down those stairs? I assumed the 'hut' Gen-san inhabited on the roof was not connected to the living space on the second floor. The 'Ogino Architecture Office' occupied the third floor as tenants. The building was constructed so that the only way to descend from the 'hut' to the ground was to use the outside staircase.

Gen-san slipped into some sandals and came outside the shop. His large feet stuck out over the edges. Those were probably Heizō-san's sandals. The small, plump Heizō-san.

Although no wind was blowing, Gen-san walked out onto the main road with a strange gait, as though he was a piece of cloth fluttering in the wind. He flapped along for a moment before his figure finally disappeared into a side street.

'*Okusan*, what do you do for a living?' Heizō-san once asked me. In recent years, about the only time I'd been asked about my job, my family situation, my place and date of birth, etcetera, was for the national census, so he took me by surprise.

'Well, I'm not an *okusan*,' I firstly established.

'Ah, sorry, sorry, so then…'

Upon being pressed like this, I let slip my surname: Karaki.

'Ah, Karaki –'

Then I blurted out my given name, too, Taeko.

'So you're Karaki Taeko-chan then,' Heizō-san said happily. From then on, Heizō-san always called me Taeko-chan. The last time anyone had added the diminutive 'chan' to my name was kindergarten. Since then with my good grades, my straight posture, and my crisp way of speaking, neither my male nor my female friends had called me Taeko-chan. *Karaki-san.* That was the name I'd been called all these years. Even my several lovers had called me Karaki-san. If they put their hearts into shattering formalities, they still only got as far as Taeko-san.

'Taeko-chan is an English teacher, you know,' Heizō-san explained, smiling, to the lady from the greengrocer's and the chicken-shop man. Before I knew it, the lady from the greengrocer's and the chicken-shop man had both started calling me Taeko-chan too.

'Yep, I hear she's a teacher at the big cram school just the next station over,' the lady from the greengrocer's said, sounding impressed, which embarrassed me.

'I'm not enough of a fool to be called "Teacher".' When I uttered that old adage, Heizō-san's face took on its usual baffled look.

'So, Tae-chan, you got anyone special in your life?' the chicken-shop man asked me. In the blink of an eye, 'Taeko-chan' had been replaced with simply 'Tae-chan.'

'No, I do not,' I said bluntly, but for some reason the chicken-shop man looked happy.

That day, I went home without buying anything from Uoharu, or Yaoyoshi, or Torikatsu. At the convenience store I put a Western-style ready meal and a vegetable juice in my basket, and went to the counter.

'Will I heat it up for you?' I was asked, and I nodded. I left the convenience store, sent off with a 'Thank you very much' in a bright voice.

I can easily shop here, without needing my surname or my given name, I thought, relieved. I hadn't had a Western-style ready meal in a long time – it was delicious.

'Tae-chan, would you think about letting someone set you up with a prospective husband?' the chicken-shop man asked, about a month after he'd asked if I had anyone special.

'No I wouldn't,' I said, without hesitation.

'That right?' said Torikatsu. 'How old are you, Tae-chan?'

'I am under no obligation to answer that,' I said briskly, and his head drooped a little. Maybe that was a bit rude, I thought, and got him to wrap up a large thigh fillet for me.

'These ones on the house,' he said, adding two yakitori skewers.

'Actually I'm 42 years old,' I said, as I was leaving, and his face lit up instantly.

'Oh, you're young, then.'

'Young?'

'Yep, thirties and forties is all middle youth to us,' he said.

Suddenly the lady from the greengrocer's was standing directly behind me. She was a sprite who appeared and disappeared unexpectedly.

'There's a deep river between your thirties and your forties,' I said.

'Even deep rivers seem like shallow brooks when you look back on them later,' said Torikatsu.

'Anyway, forget that, what do you mean by "middle youth?"' asked the lady from the greengrocer's.

'There's low youth, middle youth, and high youth. Low youth is below 30. High youth is above 50.'

'I've never heard of that,' I said, and the lady poked out her tongue.

'Everyone who passes 60 is a granny. You should leave out middle-aged lady and skip straight to granny.'

'I don't understand your logic. But Mrs Yaoyoshi, you're different from a granny. You're definitely an aunty-aged lady,' I said, and she answered, 'Hmph. But "aunty" makes me sound like a middle-aged lady, so I hate it.'

A mother and child had come into the chicken shop, and I took the opportunity to leave. Aunty from the greengrocer's left with me.

'You should let someone set you up,' she whispered in my ear.

No one special.

That was my answer, but I do have a lover of sorts. Kubota Manabu, from the same cram school. Kubota-san is five years younger than me. I married once in my twenties, and divorced two years later. I'm now a long veteran of living alone, but having divorced only last year, Kubota-san is a novice.

'What do you mean, novice?' Kubota-san always says, but I still think he's a novice. He has no problem with making offhand remarks like, it's lonely coming home with all the lights off, or, my heart aches when the theme song for *Chibi Maruko-chan* comes on TV on a Sunday night.

'The other day someone recommended that I get set up with a prospective husband,' I told Kubota-san.

'Hmmm,' he said.

Kubota-san teaches Japanese and is relatively popular at the cram school. He has a good teaching style and a natural affection for other people. After I got divorced I had relationships – of a sort – with a number of men, but among them all I'd class Kubota-san as belonging to the highest category. And that's taking into account the fact that for women, everyone apart from the man you're currently dating tends to recede into the distance.

For one, Kubota Manabu never puts on any airs. But the best thing about him is that I sleep soundly when we stay together. To explain, I can't get a wink of sleep when I'm under the same roof as someone unfamiliar to me. I thought

I was familiar enough with my ex-husband, and I married him, but gradually I grew unable to sleep by his side. When he went on the occasional work trip I would greedily sleep for about fifteen hours; a couple of nights' supply at once. That, combined with a few daytime naps here and there, was how I kept myself functioning.

Of course, when I finally brought up the subject of divorce, and gave 'I cannot sleep' as the reason, my husband wouldn't initially agree to it. So I used a video camera to record a week's worth of my nights – lying at my husband's side, wide awake and staring at the ceiling – and played it to him at four times the speed. Then he finally understood that I was serious about wanting a divorce.

'But I refused the set-up,' I told Kubota-san.

'Hmmm,' he responded in the same voice as before.

I don't have any desire to marry Kubota-san. I'm afraid of marriage, though I'm probably just being a coward to feel that way about something I only messed up once.

I see Gen-san quite often now. Well, I've probably passed him in the neighbourhood quite frequently before now without noticing. But once you get to know somebody's figure they stand out from the background and you get a grip on the shape of them.

I see Gen-san most often in the shopping street, around the pachinko[15] parlour in front of the train station. He's always empty-handed, walking in his swaying fashion. Sometimes he's just come out of the pachinko parlour and other times he's just about to go in. I ask, 'Did you win anything?' and he moves his head. He shakes it side-to-side more often than he nods it up-and-down.

Gen-san doesn't say anything. Once I asked Heizō-san if Gen-san was the type of person to hold out on you. Unusually, Heizō-san got angry.

---

15. An arcade-based gambling device, resembling a vertical pinball machine.

'No way, Gen's not the mean, petty type.'

'How is Gen-san connected to you, Heizō-san?'

'Connected? I s'pose he's, you know, like a kind of distant relative...' Heizō-san tipped up his sake bottle and slowly poured every last drop into his cup as he answered. His face had the same dazzled expression as the last time we spoke about Gen-san.

'Come to think of it, you still haven't told me who's in that photograph stuck to the wall in Uoharu.'

Heizō-san emptied his glass with relish, without answering my question. He sipped it as if savouring every single drop. When I settled the bill and left the Budō-ya, the moon had swollen to half-full, and hung at the tip of the sky.

The incident occurred in December.

The central examinations were drawing near, and the whole cram school was in a raging frenzy. One of the students attempted suicide.

It was a girl who took one of my classes. She had never taken a day off, seated herself in the front row without fail, and was always silently taking notes. I thought of her as a very earnest but somewhat unanimated child.

The student had taken sleeping tablets on the roof of the cram school. Apparently she'd secreted them away, one-by-one from her mother's prescribed medication, until she had a collection.

Kubota-san was the one who found her.

He had advised the girl many times about what schools to apply for. That day, he received a message from her saying, 'I am waiting on the roof,' so he went up to check in the evening but couldn't see her. To make sure he went to check again, past 10pm when all the lessons had finished, and the girl was leaning against the fence, unconscious. Her legs were stretched out and there was a wine bottle at her feet.

'Somehow it was so pitiful that she'd bought a half-bottle, and not a full one,' Kubota-san said with a sigh when he came back from the hospital.

Apparently the girl had tried to wash the pills down with the wine. Perhaps because she wasn't a regular drinker, not even a third of the half-bottle was gone; rather, it was the bottle of green tea placed next to the wine that was almost emptied.

'Being alive is painful,' said the suicide note, neatly folded inside a pale blue envelope and placed next to the wine bottle.

That night, Kubota-san stayed over, and I did not sleep for a second while I lay beside him. When I gave up, got out of bed and looked at the clock, it was three in the morning. I opened the curtains to gaze at the night sky and saw numerous stars. The crescent moon glowed brightly. I wondered if the girl on the rooftop had looked at the same moon.

I suddenly recalled Gen-san's face. His face outside the pachinko parlour, when he silently moved his head side-to-side or up-and-down. That was a face that had seen something, I thought, not knowing what that 'something' was. The moon looked sharp, as though it would hurt to touch it.

'How does Gen-san fit in?' I asked the lady from the greengrocer's.

The winter holiday for the regular schools had begun. School holidays are the busy periods at the cram school. At my cram school, we not only teach face-to-face, but video classes too. In this system, students can come whenever they like to watch the lessons that we have pre-recorded. Because I had to stay back after classes to put the videos together, at this time of year I did all my grocery shopping during the day. Yaoyoshi had just opened, and for a change, the lady was vague and unoccupied.

'Ah, yes,' she said slowly.

I wasn't asking with any serious intent so if we'd wandered off topic I wouldn't have minded. But the lady tilted her head to the side for a moment then said succinctly, 'Gen-san, well, he was the lover of Heizō-san's dead wife.'

'Lover,' I repeated, surprised, and the lady nodded gently. 'But, why? The lover and the husband like that.'

'Ah, well. It's a pretty famous story round these parts. So, it's not wrong for me to tell you, then,' she said, as if convincing herself. This is what she told me:

Heizō-san's wife Maki was his old childhood friend. Heizō-san graduated from university and it was decided he would continue the family business; with their parents' encouragement the two soon held their wedding. Their marriage was quite solid. At least it seemed so at first. But at some point things went wrong.

Firstly, Heizō-san's father from Uoharu died. He went out fishing and the boat capsized. The other fishermen escaped without injury; only the owner of Uoharu drowned. The water was not especially deep, nor the current flowing especially fast in that spot. It was just a terrible misfortune, everyone said, a tragedy.

Next, the mother died. She was only in her fifties, but her heart failed. She stopped breathing without ever regaining consciousness.

Maki-san's parents died the next year. They rented a car while travelling in Hokkaido. On a two-way road, they collided head-on with a driver recklessly overtaking someone from the opposite direction. Both her parents died instantly.

Such an awful run of bad luck, the people on the shopping street gossiped. And while they were still gossiping, Heizō-san's younger sister died. She joined an outing with her old high school hiking club for the long weekend in May, and met with an accident on the mountain they were climbing. Maki-san didn't have any brothers or sisters, so the couple were left completely alone.

'Now when was it…? That Maki-san switched off?'

'Switched off?' I said, and Yaoyoshi nodded.

'It's a funny way to put it, but she really did just switch off,' she said, with a look of reminiscence.

By-and-by, Maki-san met Gen-san, who was the cook at an izakaya on the edges of the neighbourhood. Something grew between them straight away.

Then, finally, Maki-san herself died around the time of her 40th birthday. She died from the same heart problems as Heizō-san's mother.

When Maki-san's funeral services had finished, Heizō-san visited Gen-san. Nobody knows what passed between them. But soon after the service for the 49th day after the death, Gen-san moved into Heizō-san's place. Some years later he quit the izakaya and took over the accounts for Uoharu. For the 20-and-a-bit years since, Gen-san had been settled in the hut on Heizō-san's roof.

It was a curious story. I didn't really think it was true. But then again, I didn't really think it was nonsense, either. It gave me a strange feeling, not least because the characters, Heizō-san and Gen-san, were actually there in front of my eyes.

Heizō-san didn't look at all like he'd been through so much. Yet, now I thought of it, I could believe that within his uncommonly affable nature there was something cold; something that makes you shiver for a moment like stepping into a cavern. Gen-san was the same, with his lanky beanpole figure, looking as though he might blow away in the wind at any minute, casually playing pachinko.

'I wonder what she's been doing since then, that girl who attempted suicide?' I tried to ask Kubota-san.

'Yeah, I heard she was checked out of the hospital, and she got much better,' Kubota-san answered in a pensive voice. It was the kind of voice you use when you can't put something into words, but the thought has always stayed in your head somewhere.

I hadn't been able to sleep in the same bed as Kubota-san since that night. *Maybe it won't work out with him either,* I fretted as I lay silently by his side.

'What will you do for Christmas, Tae-chan?' the chicken-shop man asked me.

'I'll buy a roast chicken at Torikatsu, and eat it at home,' I said courteously, and his face broke into a smile. *Does the chicken-shop man also feel anxious or scared at times?* I thought, looking at his smiling face filled with cheerful-looking wrinkles. I had no idea.

'Spend Christmas with your lover, like you're supposed to,' said the chicken-shop man, giving me two yakitori skewers on the house.

'Wait, I don't remember telling you I'm in a relationship,' I replied, surprised, and Torikatsu smiled again.

'I knew it straight away. You're so easy to read, Tae-chan.'

I headed for home, feeling light-hearted. When I exhaled, my breath was pure white. *It will probably snow tonight*, I thought.

I saw something like the true face of Heizō-san and Gen-san, just once. Uoharu was closed for the day and they were in the larger supermarket. This was the first time I had seen them together. Gen-san was pushing the trolley, and Heizō-san was swiftly throwing things into it. Plastic bags and a scrubbing brush. Milk and bamboo skewers. A few vegetables and, as I sneaked a look, two long sausages of spicy cod roe. *The shoemakers go ill-shod*, I thought, amused.

Like a married couple after many years together, they were in sync. When they stood at the spice shelves and Heizō-san picked up a large canister of pepper, Gen-san said something and the two exchanged words briefly. At some point, Gen-san clamped his mouth shut. Heizō-san also went quiet.

For a short while, they stood in silence. Not glaring at each other, but of course they didn't look intimate either.

They simply stood, staring blankly.

It reminded me of something, but I couldn't think what.

Finally, Heizō-san put the large canister of pepper back onto the shelf. Without adding a replacement item to the trolley, the two moved to a different spot. Their two faces, bereft of expression, were seared into my retina. Then the two men blended into the crowd and I lost sight of them.

Those were not expressions of mutual hatred, I realised. They were just the faces of people who had seen a lot. It was the same notion I'd had about Gen-san, that other time.

I have absolutely no desire to see 'a lot', I thought fiercely. But it's impossible to live without seeing things. I'd learnt that, unfortunately, along the way. Sometime during my life up to now.

I finally found out who was in the photograph that was pinned to the wall a few steps inside the entrance to Uoharu.

'Ah, one of them's Picasso.' Of course – I thought I'd seen that face before. It *was* Picasso. 'That other one's Jean Cocteau,' Heizō-san continued, wrapping a fillet of sashimi tuna in paper-thin shaved wood.

Stuck for words, I idiotically said, 'Wow, they're very famous.'

The small, plump man was Picasso, and the tall lanky one was Jean Cocteau. They stood and stared blankly as if neither of them was really there, like Heizō-san and Gen-san in the supermarket. That moment in the supermarket had looked exactly like the photograph pinned to the wall in Uoharu, I finally realised.

'Both of them are dead now, aren't they?'

'Yeah, are they?' said Heizō-san. There was a black lustre on the beads of the abacus that he flicked to calculate the bill. 'That's 1,200 yen,' he said, passing me the package.

The corners of the photograph of Picasso and Cocteau curled up, and because it had faded, the contrast between the black and white had grown fuzzy.

'Where did you get this photograph?' I asked, and Heizō-san tilted his head to the side.

'I wonder where I got it, eh? Can't remember…'

Gen-san emerged from out the back. As always, he was empty-handed.

'Gen, where'd I get this photo,' Heizō-san asked.

'It must have been left by Maki-san,' Gen-san answered, plainly. At the word 'Maki-san', I froze for an instant. But the two did not look as if anything was wrong. Gen-san soon flapped his way out, and Heizō-san turned to address a customer who'd just come in the shop.

'You want it?' Heizō-san said to me.

'Huh?' I responded, surprised.

'You want this photo?'

'Nope,' I said, and left Uoharu.

When I went to Uoharu two days later a beaming Heizō-san said, 'I would've given you that photo for free the other day.'

'It isn't free today?' I asked, and Heizō-san shook his head.

'I wouldn't sell it to you even for 100,000 yen.'

'Well, I wouldn't pay 100,000 yen. I wouldn't buy it for ten yen.' Since I was getting spiteful, I quickly changed the subject.

I got him to wrap up two mackerel fillets.

'Your boyfriend's coming over today, eh?' said Heizō-san.

'Why are my secrets always leaked like this?' I grumbled, and Heizō-san laughed.

'Cos you're so easy to read, Tae-chan.'

When I left Uoharu and walked off, Gen-san was in front of the pachinko parlour as usual. His fringe was mussed up in the wind, and he really did look like Cocteau in the photograph. Though a much older version of Cocteau.

I hadn't been able to sleep next to Kubota-san since that incident. But I knew that instead of breaking it off, I'd probably struggle along with him for a while longer.

You see things, even though you don't want to see them, I sang inside my head. The Cocteau of the shopping street went silently into the pachinko parlour.

An Elevator on Sunday

Shūichi Yoshida

Translated by Ginny Tapley Takemori

Lately the refuse emanating from Watanabe's flat had taken on a decidedly domestic air – apart from anything else, he'd started cooking for himself. Every Sunday night he would take the plastic bags of rubbish down in the elevator to dispose of them in the communal bins on the ground floor.

Six months earlier, he'd been sacked from his job at a shipping warehouse in Shinagawa on grounds of negligence, and then the part-time job for a removals firm he'd taken as a stopgap, which had started off as about four days a week, had dwindled to three days, then two, and for the past three weeks he hadn't had any work at all. Apparently the company didn't see anything unusual about a part-timer quitting without notice, because when he phoned to tell them and ask for his wage packet, they merely responded, 'No problem. Bring your seal and some form of ID with you, all right?' without even asking his name, much less his reason for quitting.

He had started cooking for himself to save money, of course, but then more often than not he'd spend half an hour or so making a veggie stir fry only to find that not only was it too salty but he'd forgotten to turn on the rice cooker, and would end up chucking the whole lot in the bin in disgust and then head for the nearest Chinese joint.

He didn't think it was true that guys good at cooking were popular with girls. In fact, there had been a lot more girls hanging around his flat back when he never cooked and didn't have any plates or glasses or cutlery, let alone pots or pans in the kitchen. When he first moved into this studio flat on Ikebukuro's west side, almost ten years ago now, he'd been short of storage space. Since he hadn't intended to cook anyway, he'd converted the small kitchen unit into a wardrobe by winding several layers of wire around the tap to stop it from leaking, and fixing a pole above the sink to serve as a hanger. His underwear went in the shelves, and his sweaters and trousers into the space under the sink. He'd smashed the few items of crockery he'd brought with him from the old flat and thrown them out. He didn't regret having dumped the various glasses he'd been given by the off-licence or the freebie plate from Mister Donut, or anything else for that matter.

Once he'd dispensed with the kitchen, his flat looked more like a business hotel room. Whenever he was hungry, he bought a ready-made meal from the convenience store across the street, and if he got thirsty he could always buy a bottle of oolong tea from the vending machine on the ground floor. Of course, some of the girls who had stayed over had been sweet enough to offer to cook for him, but he would tell them, 'You'll have to begin by buying a frying pan, you know,' and if they still didn't get it, he would part the shirts hanging over the sink and show them the wire wound tightly over the tap. That wired-up tap probably spoke more eloquently than any words could about his lifestyle and the type of relationship he wanted from women.

A few days after he was sacked from the Shinagawa warehouse, in a moment of lunacy he'd picked out a Teflon frying pan that caught his eye among the prizes on display at the pachinko parlour. Subsequent winnings brought him a saucepan, some plates and glasses, and he started boiling pasta and buying large bottles of oolong tea. And then three months ago he even bought himself a small rice cooker.

The day he came home from the pachinko parlour with

a frying pan, he'd boxed up all the clothes in the kitchen and removed the wire from the taps. When he removed his sweatshirts and t-shirts from the sink, he found it littered with small plastic sachets of insect repellent. He hesitantly turned on the tap, worried that having been left unused for so many years it might spurt rusty water. But the water that came out was just a little murky, and even that ran clear in no time at all.

He might have started cooking for himself, but that didn't mean his lifestyle had substantially changed in any way. He never felt bored passing the days without going to work, and while he felt a little more anxious than he had in his early twenties, at the back of his mind there was still the hope that he could find a job if he really wanted to. As he scooped out these last remnants of optimism and slowly licked them from the tip of his finger, the day would come to an end and there would be the evening's TV with non-stop baseball and comedy shows, segueing easily into the next day that had seemed so terribly distant when he'd woken that morning.

The longer he was unemployed, the more he lost the sense of what day it was, and the boundaries between yesterday, today, and tomorrow grew ever more blurred. However mixed up time became, today could only be followed by tomorrow, but then suddenly something got messed up and it wasn't tomorrow but rather yesterday again; so time passed in the utter absence of any motivation.

He began to wonder odd things, like, if time started flowing backwards, did this mean the bags of rubbish he took down to the ground floor bins every Sunday would actually be next week's rubbish? Then he would think sardonically that no, wasn't it rather that every Sunday night he was picking up somebody else's bin bags and bringing them one by one back to his flat? He glanced hastily up at the indicator light on the elevator, and saw he was indeed moving slowly but surely down from the ninth floor. If he imagined, from the vibrations in his feet, that the lift was moving downwards then it felt like it was going down. And if he imagined it going up, it felt as though it was going up.

When eventually he reached the ground floor, the caretaker's door opened and the old man came out in his pyjamas, dragging his bad leg.

'Been seeing you around a lot lately, Mr Watanabe. Out of a job, are you?' His face was flushed, as if he'd been drinking.

'Good evening,' Watanabe greeted him in return.

The old man went ahead and pushed open the door to the communal bins with his shoulder. 'You're young, so you shouldn't have any trouble finding work if you look for it,' he said with a chuckle.

'I'm not that young, you know. I'm already 30,' said Watanabe with a wry smile, as he stuffed a bag of rubbish into the bin.

'Really, 30 already?' The old man's speech started sounding unnaturally polite, although it probably had nothing to do with having just learned Watanabe's age. 'Mr. Watanabe, you were just a young man when you first moved in here, but if you don't mind my saying so, you were really quite something. The other men your age were probably students living off their parents and partying all the time, but you would be up early every morning to go to work. That always impressed me.'

Watanabe watched as the old man gave up trying to squeeze the bags into the bin, and instead made a neat pile in the corner. Come to think of it, he'd probably acquired this habit of bringing down his rubbish late on Sunday night because of one particular girl he'd been going out with a few years back. He felt a stab of nostalgia recalling all those nights when he'd brought the rubbish down as he saw her off.

He'd hooked up with Keiko two years after moving in here – or was it three? Long after wiring up the kitchen tap, of course. At the time he'd been working for a building contractor specialising in demolition. It was heavy work loading up scrap wood from the site onto the back of a lorry all day, but come evening they would finish work while it was still light and putting on a dry shirt was enough to revive him to go out on the town drinking with his mates on the day's wages. And so the days went by.

He'd met Keiko in a reggae bar on the way from his flat to Ikebukuro Station. He went there at weekends to chat up new faces at random on the basis that if he hit on enough girls he was bound to get lucky with some. In any case, they played a lot of Bob Marley and he liked the vibe there. Looking back, he couldn't remember either the girls he'd chatted up or what they'd talked about. Strangely, though, he could clearly recall the night he'd first met Keiko. Her response to his question, 'What's the place you most hate in this world?' had been 'Basement food halls in department stores.' He must have asked the same question of any number of other girls, but amongst that edgy reggae bar crowd the usual answers were along the lines of 'Disneyland' or 'Shibuya.' When he heard Keiko's answer, though, Watanabe had the feeling he'd discovered the place he himself most hated without realising it until now. 'I like the ground floor, though,' he told her. 'Just smelling all those cosmetics makes me sleepy… and when I get sleepy, I get a hard-on.'

He thought he heard Keiko snort with laughter. Sitting there in the corner of the bar, her dark skin looked moist under the UV lighting. He bought her a cocktail and moved to sit next to her.

When he pressed her over her dislike of basement food halls, her reply was simple: 'Just the thought that everyone there is thinking about eating gives me the creeps.' But Watanabe had the feeling that there was some other, more personal reason and began imagining what it might be. There must be someone in her past she didn't like eating with. She hated being watched while she was eating, and she didn't like seeing the other person eat. Maybe she felt vulnerable, as if she was being stripped naked by whoever it was staring at her while she ate. On the other hand, if she watched someone else while they were eating, she was being forced to see that person's nakedness, or listen to their pathetic whingeing.

Keiko was training to be a doctor at Yokohama Medical School, but she'd told Watanabe only that she was attending some kind of medical college, and for the first six months he had assumed she was training to be a nurse. He only found out that she was actually studying to be a doctor a few months before she sat the national medical exam. It had been the night he'd taken her to the Minakami hot spring resort to unwind since she'd seemed stressed to breaking point. She'd been embarrassed about going to the mixed open-air bath over the river, but he dragged her there anyway and embraced her in the hot water, as if deliberately showing off to the figures visible behind the hotel windows. 'I'll wash your hair for you,' he offered, showing an unusually tender side of himself, but Keiko brushed him off. 'It's too much trouble.' They sat in each other's arms in the hot water, listening to the water caressing rocks in the nearby mountain stream, illuminated by the light spilling from the hotel windows.

'It's quiet, isn't it?' Watanabe said.

'Aren't I too heavy for you?' Keiko still seemed self-conscious.

An elderly couple, who came into the bath after them, had asked, 'Are you two just married?' Watanabe couldn't recall what he'd said in reply, but after they'd gone back to the changing room and were putting on their yukata robes, he'd muttered, 'I can't believe they still have baths together at their age!' to which Keiko had replied, appalled, 'Look, the bath isn't supposed to a place for necking.' Her moist shoulder, glossy in the dim lamplight, was still etched onto his mind's eye.

It wasn't until after they'd finished dinner in their room and were sipping chilled sake by the window, picking at the remains of a little side dish, that Keiko admitted she was at medical school.

'Why didn't you tell me before?' Watanabe demanded vehemently, but he was at a loss how to respond when she replied, 'Because you never asked!' It was true. How could he have been seeing his lover every week for six months without even asking her what it was she was studying?

'But why didn't you put me right? You knew I was getting things wrong!'

'Yeah, right. Like I can really tell the kind of guy who says, "When you're a nurse you'll be able to support me. I'll make a great toy boy," that actually I'm going to be a doctor, not a nurse.'

'Oh come on, that was only a joke.'

'So looking up how much a newly qualified nurse earns was a joke too, I suppose?'

'I didn't look it up, I just happened to see it in a documentary on TV…'

It wasn't as though anything changed that night in Minakami Onsen. On the contrary, he was surprised at how indifferent he felt at hearing his girlfriend was going to be a doctor, not a nurse. It hadn't changed his feelings at all, but rather had brought home to him that something else was changing: put simply, he realised that loving someone was not a matter of gradually getting to like them more and more, but that over time it became impossible to dislike them.

Keiko would come over to his room just after lunch on Sundays. She was probably too busy with classes from Monday to Saturday, but whenever he asked her about it she teased him, 'Are you really that keen to see me?' and he backed off.

She always parked illegally on the street outside and would keep going out on the balcony to check that she hadn't been given a parking ticket. At some point he'd introduced her to the caretaker when they bumped into him by the front door, and somehow she must have won the old man over, because since then, he'd phoned them whenever he saw patrol cars out and about.

One time she'd brought a video camera with her. Watanabe had been out boozing with his mates the night before and had slept soundly until nearly noon. He'd woken briefly upon hearing the key in the front door, but having checked that it was Keiko coming into the room, he'd gone straight back to sleep. After a while she had shaken him awake with her foot and he'd opened his eyes to see her grinning and pointing a video camera at him.

He rolled over sleepily, but she climbed on the bed and started pulling the duvet off him. He tried to resist, but eventually gave up and let her do what she wanted. She pulled down his pants to film his morning erection, and laughed when he tried to twist away.

'What the fuck are you doing?' he protested, and she said, 'That's the sort of thing they're always doing in those videos you rent out, isn't it?'

He pushed her aside. 'It'd be alright if I was getting paid for it.'

'Okay, I'll pay. How much?'

'You can't afford me.'

'Just name your price.'

The figure that popped into his head was 30,000 yen, but then he thought that he'd just hit upon this as an amount she might actually pay and was disappointed with himself for being so cheap. He pulled his pants back up and grabbed the video camera, pushed her over and straddled her.

'I'll show you how I always see you.' Still atop her, he began removing her clothes. Keiko fooled around sticking out her tongue and crossing her eyes at the camera, but she didn't put up any resistance and displayed her breasts proudly as he filmed. Her body was bathed in the bright noon light streaming through the window, and rainbow reflections from the lens flickered right and left over her breasts. He slid the camera slowly up from her thighs to her belly. 'That tickles!'

she protested, goose bumps rising up on her flank as she squirmed away. He looked at her through the viewfinder, his nose brushing up against her soft skin.

'Now it's my turn. You want to know how I see you, don't you?' Stark naked, Keiko snatched the camera back and started filming him as he lay face up, angling from the crotch.

'Wow, it looks huge! Oh wait, sorry, I had the zoom on.'

They had planned to go to the cinema that afternoon, but it was already getting dark by the time they got out of bed and were heading in Keiko's car to Red Lobster for a bite to eat.

They were sitting in the restaurant stuffing their faces with lobster when one of them, he couldn't remember which, had suddenly said, 'It freaks me out when I think of that video we shot earlier sitting there,' and they'd skipped dessert and rushed back to his room. They ripped out all the tape and cut it up into little pieces, and never played at making dirty films of themselves again. Yet the feel of the goose bumps on Keiko's skin that time still lingered in Watanabe's fingertips.

Returning to his room after seeing Keiko off in her car, he would sometimes be startled by an image of her having an accident on the way home. Having just watched her drive off, the scene of her car smashing head-on into a lorry as she took the turn for Kanamechō at the big junction on Ikebukuro's west side, would pop into his head with such force that he actually felt the shock of the impact. It wasn't unusual to be worried about your lover driving home, but in Watanabe's egotistical fantasy he had the urge to rush to be the first at the scene of the accident and pull Keiko, covered in blood, from the wreckage. If there was no hope of saving her, rather than watch her writhe in agony, he would strangle her with his own hands to put her out of her misery. As the fantasy ballooned in his mind, he would snort with laughter and brush his teeth harder, telling himself that, of course, Keiko hadn't had an accident. Even so, the image of her lying in the road covered in blood would not dissipate until she called to tell him she'd arrived home safely.

Once he'd told her about this half in jest, and she too had taken it as a joke.

'Even if you think you can't save me, take me to the hospital anyway, okay?' she told him, laughing.

'But wouldn't you rather I killed you than die in a car crash?' he teased, but she sounded more like a doctor when she responded, 'Dying isn't that dramatic, you know.'

'You're such a sweet girl. Not.'

'So "a sweet girl" is one who wants to be killed by her lover?'

He wondered how long it had taken him to stop imagining her being in an accident.

Around the time Keiko was busy studying for her exams and couldn't come round any more, Watanabe walked out of his job at the demolition firm. Of course, his resignation was due to his habitual laziness and had nothing to do with her exams, and when he stopped going to work he started going to the pachinko parlour again. It was obvious that overall he ended up out of pocket, but whenever his takings were up at the end of the day he would get the urge to throw caution to the wind and find himself heading for the alley behind the station's north exit where all the foreign whores hung out.

One time, he'd just started walking down the street with a hungry look on his face when a dark, big-bottomed woman called out to him in broken Japanese.

'I can't afford a hotel, so the emergency staircase'll do,' he said, to show he knew the ropes.

Her expression hardened. 'You're not a cop, are you?' she asked.

'Course not. A cop wouldn't be in this state, now, would he?' He took the woman's hand with its red-painted nails and held it to his crotch. She took him to the emergency staircase of an office block occupied by various businesses. The landings were all occupied by other couples, and in the end they had to climb up to the top of the metal stairs before they could find one vacant. She knelt down before him and he watched as her fingers deftly undid his belt. Thrusting rhythmically against her hot tongue, the vision of Keiko studying hard at home came into his mind. *Of course, you have to cram a lot of knowledge into your head to become a doctor*, he thought, impressed, as he might be with a complete stranger.

An argument broke out on the landing below, between a prostitute and a man who didn't want to pay. It sounded like a dogfight, with his drunken slurring words and her broken Japanese.

Watanabe finally met up with Keiko again several weeks later, after she'd finally finished her exams. She looked as if her nerves – strung taut as a bow all this time – had finally snapped, and for some reason Watanabe had the impression his feelings for her had cooled.

At random moments, walking down the street or having dinner, she would mutter, 'I just hope I passed,' and he would respond slickly, 'Don't worry, of course you have.' She'd staked her life on these exams, but to tell the truth he couldn't really care less whether she'd passed or not – and this indifference was quite unlike what he'd felt upon learning she was studying to become a doctor and not a nurse, or so he was beginning to think.

They had planned to travel abroad when her exams were over, but now that Watanabe was unemployed he didn't know how he was going to pay next month's rent, let alone go on holiday. When he didn't even glance at the travel brochures Keiko brought with her, she suddenly seemed even more determined to go and, since he kept insisting that he was skint, eventually she said she would pay for him. He wasn't so macho as to reject the idea of a woman paying for him to have fun, but neither would he stoop to being overjoyed at her offer.

They never had a real fight in all the time they were together, save for just one occasion when he shouted at her. It was after Keiko learned she'd passed the national exam with flying colours and commented, 'So that's my future settled at last. Now let's see about you.' For some reason he had overreacted, yelling, 'What the fuck has it got to do with you?' so loudly even he had been shocked. He had often joked around, saying things like 'I should put on my CV that my girlfriend's a doctor,' and they'd both laugh, and Keiko herself had never talked about the future in any particularly deep sense. Still, after he raised his voice at her, the strained atmosphere between them took some time to go back to normal. They both seemed to realise that what they'd always taken as jokes weren't really jokes at all, and actually they'd just been pretending that they hadn't known this all along.

Now that Keiko was in her foundation year of training, she was working Monday to Friday at the university hospital and weekend nights at various other hospitals around the city, and had hardly any time off. Even when she did make the effort to arrange to meet, often some emergency would come up and she'd have to go back to work. To begin with, Watanabe would be annoyed whenever she cancelled at the last moment, but he soon got used to it and whenever she called to say, 'Sorry, but it looks like I won't be able to make it,' he'd immediately get on the phone to someone else: 'Hi, sorry it's such short notice, but I'm free today.'

'Maybe we should split up.'

It was Watanabe who first brought this up, but it was apparent that it had occurred to Keiko too, although she seemed to be against the idea, saying, 'I reckon it'll take me just a bit longer to get used to things, and then I'll have a bit more time…' It probably didn't help that she was only getting about three hours sleep a night, and as soon as he started talking about breaking up, she would be breathing deep and evenly, fast asleep in his arms. If she'd been the sort of woman to say something like, 'Lovers are supposed to stand by their partner when the going gets tough, aren't they?' he wouldn't have had any qualms about leaving her, but gazing at her face after she'd fallen asleep out of sheer exhaustion, he would have the feeling that too much had been left unsaid. He tried shaking her awake, but found the only words that came out of his mouth were, 'Maybe we should split up.'

Things had been going on like this for a while when a good friend of his was arrested for possession of cannabis, and although Watanabe himself had nothing to do with it, his room was twice raided by police. He didn't feel like going home to that mess, so he couch-surfed for a while.

At the end of September, Keiko had a week off work and, without even asking, Watanabe about his plans, bought two tickets to San Francisco. Seeing her beaming at him, Watanabe couldn't help feeling that this really was the end. There was no denying that their relationship had been reduced to him waiting around on some vague promise of going away together, and Keiko herself seemed to be trying to put things right by going on this trip.

'We need to talk,' he told her.

She was in her underwear, about to get in the shower. 'Right now? I feel all sweaty and gross. Can't it wait until after I've got clean?'

He had already put off talking about splitting up for so long that it couldn't hurt to wait another ten minutes. He flopped down on the bed and stared at the ceiling. After a while he noticed her handbag beside him on the bed where she'd thrown it down, and he picked it up and threw it up to the ceiling and caught it again, threw it up and caught it. When the handbag was within inches of the ceiling it seemed to stop for a moment in mid-air. He carried on doing this for a while, until he missed and the bag bounced off the corner of the bed and landed on the floor, spilling its contents.

The plane tickets she'd shown him earlier lay under the table. He reached out his hand for them, thinking he'd have another look, and then noticed Keiko's passport lying there alongside them. It was Korean. He opened it up and saw Keiko's photograph, her cheeks still plump, alongside some Hangul characters that he couldn't read but which he supposed spelled out her name. So Keiko was Korean! It came as a bit of a shock, but then, come to think of it, she always had kind of looked like a Korean beauty, he thought, as he flipped through the stamp-crammed pages.

The sound of the shower stopped, and Keiko came out of the bathroom with a towel wrapped round her.

'I never knew you were Korean,' he told her, waving the open passport at her. She froze, but quickly recovered herself and smiled.

'It's not like I ever tried to hide it from you.'

Realising it was probably a touchy subject for her, he tried to lighten things up, saying, 'How long ago was that photo taken? You look fatter in it.'

Keiko started drying her hair, but then remembered, 'Oh. Wasn't there something you wanted to talk to me about?'

'Ah, right...' Given the timing, he couldn't bring himself to raise the subject of splitting up now. He had never thought of himself as discriminatory in any way, but wouldn't scrapping the conversation he wanted to have *because* of the situation also be a form of discrimination? Nevertheless, he came out with something else altogether.

'It's nothing important – just that today I came across some weird kids in the pachinko parlour car park.'

'Weird kids?'

'Well not weird, exactly. The older one was about nine, and his little brother was maybe six or so. They were the spitting image of each other. You know that pachinko parlour I always go to near the West Exit? They were standing there in the car park.'

'Weren't they just waiting for their Mum or Dad to finish playing pachinko? Not really all that weird.'

'Maybe so, but... I'd just got some chocolate as part of

my winnings, so I gave it to them. I suppose they must have been waiting, but they looked hungry, and they almost fought over the chocolate, stuffing it into their mouths until their cheeks were bulging.'

The sweet fragrance of the moisturiser Keiko was spreading on her skin wafted over to the bed. Her face, as she glanced at Watanabe putting the passport and air tickets back in her bag, was reflected in the mirror.

He didn't tell her, but that evening, after giving the kids the chocolate, Watanabe had asked the young brothers if they were hungry. The younger boy, his cheeks still full of chocolate, nodded meekly, but the older one glared at Watanabe with wary eyes, and grabbed his brother's hand as if ready to make a run for it at any moment. He must have gripped it quite hard, for the younger boy grimaced and twisted away, trying to shake his hand free. It was then that he noticed the sour smell coming from their bodies, as if they hadn't had a bath for several days. Looking closer, he saw they were both carrying backpacks and looked completely worn out.

'Is your Dad in there? Or your Mum?' he asked, making his voice as gentle as he could, and the younger boy shook his head, but the older boy nodded hastily as if to correct him, and said forcefully, 'Yes.'

'So which is it?' asked Watanabe, laughing. 'You guys look hungry. Where are you from? Do you live around here?' The pair seemed about to say something, but just continued looking at him with anguished faces as if they couldn't get the words out.

'See that takoyaki[16] stall over there?' Watanabe said. 'If I buy some for you too, will you go and get it for me? It's really tasty, but it looks like the old man's there today and I don't get on with him.'

He kept his tone deliberately light. The pair looked in unison over at the stall on the other side of the street.

If these boys had run away from home, thought

Watanabe, then he could understand what kind of things would make them trust an adult's words, and what would make them wary. After all, children ran away from home for a reason. Come to think of it, Keiko never talked about her family to him. That was probably the biggest difference between her and all the other girls he had ever been out with: she had never talked about her own family, nor asked Watanabe about his either.

The two boys kept glancing over Watanabe's shoulder at the takoyaki stall. Then they looked at each other, and appeared to be communicating something between them just with their eyes.

'If you don't want to, that's fine. I can ask someone else.'

Watanabe started putting his money back into his wallet, but the older boy nervously stretched out his hand. Watanabe pressed a couple of notes into his hand.

'Get three portions, one for each of us. And some juice, too,' he said, giving their little backs a push. As they waited for the dumplings filled with octopus chunks to finish cooking, the pair glanced repeatedly over their shoulders back at Watanabe.

They came back with three packs of takoyaki and three cans of juice, just as they'd been told, and sat next to each other on a wheel block in the car park. Watanabe watched quietly as, without saying a word, they blew onto the hot food to cool it before eating. He could easily take them to the nearest police box, but he didn't think that would solve anything. The older boy finished eating first, and Watanabe handed him his own pack virtually untouched. The boy studied his face for a few moments, then snatched it from him. At his side, his younger brother hastily took a gulp of juice to wash down the food in his mouth, and held out his hand for his share.

---

16. A ball-shaped battered snack, typically filled with octopus (*tako*).

When Watanabe stood up to leave, the older boy took the change from the takoyaki from his pocket and held it out to him.

'That's okay, keep it.'

Watanabe left the car park and walked for a while. He'd intended to go straight to exchange his pachinko winnings for cash, but he couldn't shake the boys from his mind. Eventually he went back to the pachinko parlour car park, but they had already gone. All that remained was the empty packs smeared with seaweed powder and sauce.

That night, after making love with Keiko for the first time in ages, when she went to the bathroom to rinse out her mouth, he asked her, 'Hey, didn't you once tell me that you hate watching people eat?'

Apparently his voice didn't reach her, because she said, 'What? Did you say something?'

Ignoring her, he went on, 'Today I watched them – those two boys – eating takoyaki, and I didn't feel that way at all, quite the opposite in fact. Watching them, I felt really happy…'

'What? I can't hear you.'

She came back into the room and, still naked, sat on the edge of the bed, took a bottle of mineral water from the table, and drank from it. Watanabe put his hand on her thigh and, still drinking, she twisted away from him.

She got back into bed, and he pillowed her head on his arm. 'What were you saying just now?' she asked again, and he answered just, 'Nothing important,' and dozed off. After a while, he heard Keiko ask in a small voice, 'Hey, you're not upset about it, are you?'

'About what?' he asked sleepily.

'About my passport.'

'Not at all.'

His arm was beginning to go numb. He tried to take it from under her head, but she held on to it tightly, 'Just a little longer.'

At the end of summer, he and Keiko went on the trip to San Francisco. They stayed for seven days and five nights, during which time he relied on Keiko's fluency in English for everything.

For sometime afterwards, too, they carried on meeting once a week or sometimes not even that. Even though she smiled at him the way she'd always done, at some point, she started calling less and less, and Watanabe himself didn't even notice.

Soon after coming back from the trip, she'd asked him if he wanted to try working at her father's restaurant in Shibuya, but he'd turned her down on some trivial pretext such as not being much good at dealing with customers. She hadn't pressed him on it any further.

How many years had it been since he had last heard from her? He had often thought of calling, but he didn't have anything in particular to say to her, and he never got as far as picking up the phone. The only change in his life since he'd last seen her was that he'd returned his clothes shelf to its original role as a kitchen.

Just once, not long ago, he'd caught sight of her at a hospital.

That night, he had been out drinking with a friend who worked on the reception at a telephone dating club. The friend had got drunk and started pestering some students at the next table, which led to some trouble between them. Watanabe and some of the staff had intervened and managed to quieten them down, but after they'd paid, while Watanabe went off to the toilet, his friend had gone outside to find the students waiting for him. By the time Watanabe had staggered up the stairs to the street, his friend was already curled up in a protective ball on the ground surrounded by students giving him a thorough kicking. Somebody must have already reported it because Watanabe had just waded in to break it up when two cops arrived. The friend was loaded into an ambulance with a broken tooth and his hand pressed over one eye, his chin and sweatshirt stained dark with blood.

While his friend was being treated in the hospital, Watanabe sat alone in the dimly-lit waiting room. He heard footsteps of someone approaching along the dark corridor, and automatically glanced in their direction. Silhouetted in the light before the elevator, wearing a white coat and slightly thinner, with her hair cut slightly shorter than before, was Keiko. He stood up from the bench to talk to her, but just then a voice rang out, 'Doctor, you forgot this!' and a nurse came down the corridor after her. Keiko took a slim file from the nurse and then got into the elevator. Her shoulders were drooping and she looked worn out.

The elevator with Keiko in it went slowly up. He half expected her to stop at the ninth floor, but she carried on steadily up to the very top.

About the Authors

Born in 1964, **Kaori Ekuni** came to prominence initially as the author of young adults' books before garnering several awards for her short fiction – taking the Yamamoto Shūgorō Prize in 2002 for *Oyogu no ni Anzen de mo Tekisetsu de mo Arimasen* ('Not Safe or Suitable for Swimming'), and the Naoki Prize in 2004 for *Gokyu Suru Junbi wa Dekite Ita* ('I Was Already Prepared to Wail in Lament'). Her novels include *Kirakira Hikaru* ('Twinkle Twinkle') published in 1991, and *Hoyo, Arui wa Raisu ni wa Shio O* ('To Embrace, or to Pour Salt on the Rice', 2010), which is now regarded as one of her most important works.

Hideo Furukawa was born in 1966 and is highly regarded for the richness of his storytelling and his willingness to experiment; chameleon-like, he changes his style with every new book. His best-known novel is the 2008 *Seikazoku* ('Holy Family'), an epic work of alternate history set in northeastern Japan, where he was born. His 2011 *Umatachi yo, Soredemo Hikari wa Muku de* ('O Horses! At Least The Light Remains Pure'), written after Furukawa visited the area devastated by the Great East Japan Earthquake of 2011, is considered a sequel.

Osamu Hashimoto was born in 1948. He graduated from the University of Tokyo and worked as an illustrator before becoming a writer. He has published fiction, literary criticism and essays as well as modern Japanese translations of classics such as *The Tale of Genji*, turning out numerous bestsellers. Hashimoto received the Kobayashi Hideo Prize in 2002 for *Mishima Yukio to wa Nanimono Datta no Ka* ('Who Was Yukio

Mishima?'), a work of criticism. In 2005 he won the Shibata Renzaburo Award for his short story collection *Cho no Yukue* ('Where Butterflies Go').

Toshiyuki Horie, a scholar of French literature, is a Professor at Waseda University. As epitomised by his novel *Kuma no shikiishi* ('The Bear and the Paving Stone', translated into French as *Le Pavé de l'Ours*), which won the Akutagawa Prize, his writing probes the area between truth and fiction, straddling the line between essays reflecting on his own experiences and straight fiction. In 2003 he won the Kawabata Yasunari Prize for the short story *Sutansu Dotto* ('Approach Dots'), and in 2004 the Tanizaki Jun'ichiro Prize for the collection *Yukinuma to Sono Shuhen* ('Yukinuma and its Environs'). He has received the Yomiuri Prize for Literature twice: for his 2005 novel *Kagan Bojitsu Sho* ('Riverbank Days'), and for 2009's *Seigen Kyokusen* ('Sine Wave') in the essay category.

Hitomi Kanehara was born in Tokyo in 1983. She dropped out of high school at the age of 15 to pursue her passion for writing, with the support of her father, Mizuhito Kanehara, a literary professor and translator of children's literature. She wrote her first novel *Hebi ni Piasu* ('Snakes and Earrings') at the age of 21. The novel won the prestigious Akutagawa Prize and the Subaru Literary Prize. Her other works include *Autofiction* (Shueisha Publishing Co., 2006), and *Hydra* (Shincho Publishing Co., 2007).

Hiromi Kawakami was born in Tokyo and graduated from Ochanomizu Women's College in 1980. Her first book was a collection of short stories entitled *Kamisama* ('God') published in 1994. In 1996 she won the prestigious Akutagawa Award for *Hebi a Fumu* ('Tread on a Snake'). Her novel *Sensei no Kaban* ('The Briefcase') won the 2001 Tanizaki Prize and was shortlisted for the 2012 Man Asian Literary Prize. Published in the UK as *Strange Weather in Tokyo* (trans. Allison Markin Powell), it was shortlisted for the Independent Foreign Fiction Prize, 2014.

Nao-Cola Yamazaki is a Japanese writer, born in 1978. Her debut novella *Don't Laugh at People's Sex Lives* won the 2004 Bungei Prize. Since then she has written more than ten novels, as well as several essay collections. Her work has appeared in translation in *Words Without Borders* and Asymptote. Her real name is Naoko; she chose her pen name because she really loves Diet Coke.

Mitsuyo Kakuta's debut novel, *Kofuku na Yugi* ('A Blissful Pastime'), received the Kaien Prize for New Writers in 1990. She won the prestigious Naoki Prize for the second half of 2004 with *Taigan no Kanojo* ('Woman on the Other Shore'), and the Chuo Koron Literary Prize in 2007 with *Yokame no Semi* ('The Eighth Day'), which was made into a televised drama series and a film. The book sold more than a million copies. In 2012 she won the Shibata Renzaburo Award for her novel *Kami no Tsuki* ('Paper Moon'), and the Izumi Kyoka Prize for her volume of short stories *Kanata No Ko* ('The Children Beyond').

Banana Yoshimoto, born in 1964, may be second only to Haruki Murakami in overseas name recognition among Japanese writers today. Her works have been translated and published in over 30 countries. In Italy she has received the Scanno Prize (1993), the Fendissime Prize (1996), the Maschera d'argento Prize (1999), and the Capri Award (2011). Her father was the noted critic and poet Takaaki Yoshimoto (1924-2012), her mother Kazuko (1927-2012) was a haiku poet, and her older sister is the manga artist Yoiko Haruno. Yoshimoto made her literary debut shortly after graduating from college by winning the 1987 Kaien Prize for New Writers for the novella *Kitchen* (tr. 1993).

Shūichi Yoshida was born in Nagasaki, and studied Business Administration at Hosei University. He won the Bungakukai Prize for New Writers in 1997 for his story *Saigo no Musuko*, and the Akutagawa Prize in 2002 for *Park Life*. In 2002 he also won the Yamamoto Shūgorō Prize for *Parade*. His 2007 novel, *Akunin*, won the Osaragi Jiro Prize and the Mainichi Publishing Culture Award, and was recently adapted into an award-winning 2010 film by Lee Sang-il.

About the Translators

Dan Bradley is a writer and translator. He read English at Cambridge University and has previously worked as a rowing coach in Australia, an English teacher in Japan and an editor for the EU in Spain. Dan was an editorial intern on Granta's special issue of new Japanese writing, and is a review contributor for *New Welsh Review*, *Planet, Review 31* and *The Times Literary Supplement*.

Lucy Fraser is a Lecturer in Japanese at The University of Queensland, Australia. She has a PhD in fairy tale transformations in Japanese and English, which was partly researched in Tokyo. Her other translations include a story by Hoshino Tomoyuki and literary criticism by Honda Masuko and Fujimoto Yukari.

Morgan Giles is a translator, reviewer and writer. She has translated works by authors including Naocola Yamazaki, Gen'ichiro Takahashi, and Fumiko Hayashi, and her reviews have appeared in the *Times Literary Supplement* and at *For Books' Sake* and *Full Stop.* Originally from Kentucky, she lives in London.

Hart Larrabee grew up in the United States but has lived in Japan for most of his adult life. In addition to literature, he translates in the fields of art, design, architecture, market research, branding, and whatever else crosses his desk.

Jonathan Lloyd-Davies is a translator of Japanese fiction. His translations include Edge by Koji Suzuki, with co-translator Camellia Nieh, the Demon Hunters trilogy by Baku

Yumemakura, Gray Men by Tomotake Ishikawa, and NanCore by Mahokaru Numata.

Samuel Malissa is studying Japanese Literature at Yale University. His research concerns the history of translation out of Japanese and representations of Japan through translated media.

Lydia Moëd studied Japanese at Cambridge, and later did an MA in Theory and Practice of Translation at SOAS, University of London. In addition to being a translator, she is also a literary agent and translation rights specialist. She currently lives in Toronto.

Takami Nieda has translated Hiroshi Yamamoto's The *Stories of Ibis* (2010), Sayuri Ueda's *The Cage of Zeus* (2011), as well as art books for Studio Ghibli films. In addition to working as a translator and screenwriter, Nieda teaches American studies and translation at Sophia University in Tokyo, Japan.

Ginny Tapley Takemori studied Japanese at the universities of SOAS (London), Waseda (Tokyo), and Sheffield, and has translated a dozen or so early modern and contemporary Japanese authors, including *From the Fatherland with Love* by Ryū Murakami, *Puppet Master* by Miyuki Miyabe, and *The Whale that Fell In Love with a Submarine* by Akiyuki Nosaka.

Asa Yoneda was born in Osaka and became bilingual at the age of two. She studied Japanese and translation at Oxford and SOAS, and translates fiction with a preference for experimental writing and women's writing. She lived in Tokyo for ten years and now lives in Bristol.

ALSO AVAILABLE IN THIS SERIES...

The Book of Rio

978-1905583577

Edited by Toni Marques & Katie Slade

Featuring:

João Ximenes Braga, Cesar Cardoso, Nei Lopes, Patrícia Melo, Marcelo Moutinho, João Gilberto Noll, Domingos Pellegrini, Luiz Ruffato, Sérgio Sant'Anna, and Elvira Vigna.

The Book of Gaza

978-1905583645

Edited by Atef Abu Saif

Featuring:

Atef Abu Saif, Abdallah Tayeh, Talal Abu Shawish, Mona Abu Sharekh, Najlaa Ataallah, Ghareeb Asqalani, Nayrouz Qarmout, Yusra al Khatib, Asmaa al Ghul & Zaki al 'Ela.

The Book of Istanbul

978-1905583317

Edited by Gul Turner & Jim Hinks

Featuring:

Nedim Gursel, Mehmet Zaman Saçlioglu, Muge Iplikci, Murrat Gülsoy, Sema Kaygusuz, Turker Armaner, Özen Yula, Mario Levy, Gönül Kivilcim & Karin Karakasli.

The Book of Liverpool

978-1905583096

Edited by Maria Crossan & Eleanor Rees

Featuring:

Ramsey Campbell, Lucy Ashley, Dinesh Allirajah, Frank Cottrell Boyce, Margaret Murphy, Eleanor Rees, Tracy Aston, Beryl Bainbridge, Paul Farley, James Friel, Clive Barker & Brian Patten.

The Book of Leeds

978-1905583010

Edited by Maria Crossan & Tom Palmer

Featuring:

Martyn Bedford, Jeremy Dyson, Ian Duhig, Andrea Semple, M.Y. Alam, Tom Palmer, Susan Everett, David Peace, Shamshad Khan & Tony Harrison.